DISENGAGED

Recent Titles by Mischa Hiller

SABRA ZOO
SHAKE OFF
DISENGAGED *

* *available from Severn House*

DISENGAGED

Mischa Hiller

This first world edition published 2015
in Great Britain and the USA by
SEVERN HOUSE PUBLISHERS LTD of
19 Cedar Road, Sutton, Surrey, England, SM2 5DA.
Trade paperback edition first published 2015 in Great
Britain and the USA by SEVERN HOUSE PUBLISHERS LTD.

Hiller, Mischa author.
  Disengaged.
  1. Computer software industry–Fiction. 2. Suspense
fiction.
  I. Title
  823.9'2-dc23

ISBN-13: 978-0-7278-8473-2 (cased)
ISBN-13: 978-1-84751-557-5 (trade paper)
ISBN-13: 978-1-78010-604-5 (e-book)

All Severn House titles are printed on acid-free paper.

Severn House Publishers support the Forest Stewardship Council™ [FSC™],
the leading international forest certification organisation. All our titles that
are printed on FSC certified paper carry the FSC logo.

Typeset by Palimpsest Book Production Ltd.,
Falkirk, Stirlingshire, Scotland.
Printed and bound in Great Britain by
TJ International, Padstow, Cornwall.

This book is dedicated to the memory of Paul Westlake,
a trusted reader and all-round good egg.

ACKNOWLEDGEMENTS

Thanks to Professor Andrew Dempster, Sarah Dobbs, Will Frazer and Azadeh Moaveni for helping me with research for the book.

ONE

Europeans could no more tell a Turk from an Iranian, Mojgan thought, than she could distinguish an English person from an American, just by looking at them. That's why she'd had no problem at the airport, travelling on a German passport with a Turkish name.

She was sitting in a fast-food restaurant in St Pancras railway station, London, watching the rapid flow of people outside on the concourse. The chicken she'd ordered sat untouched in front of her, the nausea caused by the greasy smell quelled only slightly by the weak coffee they were fond of serving in Europe. They compensated for taste with volume, and served it in ever larger cups. Only in Turkey had she been served decent coffee, but that didn't really count; that was still within the realms of civilisation. It was late afternoon and just twenty minutes since she'd arrived on a train from Luton airport. She was tired after her four-hour flight from Bodrum in Turkey, which had been preceded by a forty-hour overland trip from Tehran which had taken nearly three days with stops.

On her smart phone – containing a new SIM card she'd activated on the train – she started an app that allowed you to play a version of online Scrabble. With practised thumbs she logged in as 'Mawlana' and keyed the username 'Shamsuddin' into the 'Invite to Play' box. As she waited for a response she looked out at the busy station concourse. Her first visit to England had so far been limited to the transport system. Soon she would have to venture into the city of London, and a period of decompression seemed like a good idea. A soft tone meant that her invitation to a new game had been accepted by Shamsuddin. A set of random letters appeared at the bottom of the screen. She placed three of them on the board to create a basic word. Only five points scored. She waited. A new notification appeared telling her that her opponent had sent her a private message. She smiled and touched it with her finger.

Are you ready for a new game? it read.

Only if you are you ready to lose, she typed.

Shall we agree no dictionary? came the reply.

Agreed. No dictionary. With the prearranged authentication over with, she waited. At another table an overweight man in a suit, Asian by the look of him, was staring at her as he pushed fries into his mouth. She wasn't wearing her headscarf, although her hair, as always when she was in public without it, was tied back, and she was dressed in a grey trouser suit, just another woman travelling on business. Mojgan had learnt through experience that, on the whole, wearing the scarf in Europe attracted more attention than not wearing it. She wasn't sure which was worse: the openly appraising stare she was now ignoring, which every male thought was his right to indulge in, or the curious and sometimes hostile ones she attracted when she had it on. Since, in her current setting, she felt more invisible without it, and her job was, after all, to remain invisible, she kept it in her bag. It came in useful when needing to gain the trust of Muslim contacts in Europe, some of whom, especially the men, confused a love of the Almighty with piety and fervour. In some ways they could be worse than the people back home, so when their initial surprise at having to deal with a woman was replaced with a realization of whom she represented, they became obsequious. It was a moment she had come to relish, that switch from derision to deference.

She looked down at her phone. Her opponent, his beautiful face still fresh in her mind, had laid a six-letter word across hers and scored twenty-seven points. She smiled and typed, *Are you cheating?*

A delay, during which she worried that she'd strayed from the script, but then her remark was quite innocent to any possible eavesdropper. Then the message came back: *No! My english is improving ;-)*

She played another word, this time scoring nine points. Soon the expected SMS text appeared: just a message that said *supper is ready*. She went back to the word game and typed, *I am going shopping now; I will continue this game tomorrow.*

OK, came the reply, *I hope you find what you need.* Again she smiled. She could picture Farsheed's face, four hours ahead, somewhere in Azerbaijan. He'd told her it had become the new front line against the Zionists.

She logged out of the app and checked her make-up in a small mirror taken from her voluminous handbag. When putting it back she made sure, for the millionth time, that she still had the cash she'd recovered from the suitcase lining after passing through customs. She then took a piece of paper from a pad and wrote down a memorized address. She had associated the number and street name with various physical objects to make it easier. She left her meal uneaten and wheeled her small case out on to the concourse, then outside into what passed in England for heat, judging by the bare legs and arms of the women, to whom nobody seemed to pay much heed. After a short wait at the taxi rank she got into the back of one of those black London cabs she'd seen in films and held the piece of paper against the glass screen so the driver could read the address. She wasn't confident that she would pronounce it properly.

'First time in London, love?'

'Yes.' Had he just called her 'love'?

'Business or pleasure?'

'Business,' she said.

She sat back where the driver couldn't see her in his rearview mirror and ripped up the address, after which she gradually let the pieces out of the window in dribs and drabs. She tried to relax. She would feel much happier when the job was done and she was on her way back home, where Farsheed would have returned from his own mission and could comb his fingers through her unbound hair.

TWO

The doctor, a male somewhere in his fifties, looked suitably attired for someone charging Julian hundreds of pounds per consultation, not including all the tests he'd had. Julian reckoned the doctor's suit had cost him two sessions, the shoes another. The doctor looked at Julian over frameless reading glasses, a piece of paper held in both hands, his elbows on the heavyweight wooden desk. There was even a blotter on the table, for Christ's sake, and an ultra-sleek laptop to one side which was presumably designed to convey to patients that their doctor was up to date with technology but wouldn't let it come between him and his patients.

'There's nothing in the results to indicate any anomalies,' he said. He glanced down at the sheet before him and shook his head. 'No, everything looks fine.' It seemed to Julian that he'd wanted to add 'as usual', but £300 of professionalism had curbed his tongue.

'So where next?' asked Julian, shifting in the leather armchair. Maybe Dr Banerjee was too old fashioned. Maybe Julian needed a younger doctor aware of new scientific approaches that had bypassed Banerjee. The doctor put the results down on an open file and took off his glasses, folding them a little too affectedly for Julian's liking before placing them above the file on the pristine blotter.

'Well, where would you like to go next?' he asked.

Julian deliberately frowned, asking, 'Isn't that *your* job, Dr Banerjee?', keeping the stress on 'your' just the right side of sarcasm. Dr Banerjee sighed and his shoulders slumped as he did so. He wiped a hand down his face and revealed a different man.

'You've been coming here for' – he consulted the file in front of him – 'for nearly six months now and I've found nothing wrong with you. We've run various heart tests, you've had an endoscopy, a colonoscopy, X-rays, numerous blood tests and, if memory serves, a liver biopsy. The most I can find wrong is irritable bowel syndrome and slightly elevated liver enzymes; in line with most of the population, in fact. The truth is, much as I'd like to keep taking your money, I don't think there's much point to more tests. I'd be lying to you if I thought them necessary.' Julian sat through this without reacting. He looked at the fat fountain pen that Dr Banerjee was caressing with his chubby fingers.

'So there's nothing you can do for me?'

The doctor stopped caressing the pen and put his fingers together. 'Well, there is one approach left to explore,' he said. 'But it depends how open you are to it.'

'I don't know until I hear what it is, but I'm not into any New Age mumbo-jumbo,' Julian said. Dr Banerjee put his glasses back on, took the cap off his fountain pen and scratched something on a pad. He typed briefly into his laptop, peered at the screen, then scratched some more. He ripped the sheet from his pad and passed it to Julian.

'She's the best in her field. My recommendation is that you go and see her.'

Julian took the sheet and looked at the name and a London telephone number.

'She sees her private patients in Bloomsbury,' the doctor said, as if to reassure Julian that she was too classy to have a surgery in Harley Street, where hundreds of doctors rented rooms so they could use the prestigious address for their private practice.

'What's her specialty then?' Julian asked, studying the name as if it would tell him. Dr Banerjee put his elbows on the table, and his hands together as if in prayer. He hadn't removed his glasses, so he lowered his chin to look at Julian over the top of the frames.

'Have you considered the possibility, Mr Fisher, that your problems could be psychosomatic in nature?'

THREE

An hour after leaving Harley Street Julian was sitting in his business partner's office in north London. Rami, who was dressed in a more stylishly modern suit than Dr Banerjee but without a tie, sat knee-to-knee opposite. They had adjacent offices overlooking the open-plan area where the software development team worked. Glass-fronted, so that, according to Rami, less of a perceived barrier existed between management and workers at Hadfish Systems (an amalgamation of their surnames, Haddad and Fisher, had seemed like a good idea all those years ago). As it was, Julian spent a lot of his time sitting next to one of the software developers in the open-plan area, as he liked to keep his hand in, although Rami told him he was micromanaging. But then Rami didn't really understand project management, or coding for that matter.

'Everything all right at the doctor's?' he asked, swivelling from the waist down in his hi-tech chair. Rami had his desk against the wall because he said he wanted nothing between him and anyone popping in to see him. Julian had his facing the door, and, unlike Rami's glass slab, had something he could sit behind. A bit like Dr Banerjee, now that he thought about it.

'Fine. Everything's fine. Just a checkup.'

'Good. Good.' He got up and closed his door. The last time he'd done that was the day after Julian had taken ill in the office, believing he was having a heart attack. Paramedics had been called but they'd left, claiming it was a panic attack. Luckily everyone apart from Rami had already gone home. The next morning he'd ushered Julian into this office, closed the door, and insisted he go and see someone privately as the NHS were not to be trusted; all they cared about was keeping him from occupying a precious bed. So it was on Rami's recommendation that he'd first gone to see Dr Banerjee in Harley Street, a man who now believed Julian's symptoms were all in his mind.

'Listen, Jules, I think I'm on to something that might, just might, take us to a different level.'

'Oh, yes?' Julian was used to Rami's hyperbole, although he seemed more excited than usual. He was the sales side of the company, relentlessly chasing clients, doing presentations, pitching for jobs, submitting tenders. Julian did help with some of these things, especially on the technical side, but he was primarily responsible for developing the software they sold. Over the last ten years they had carved themselves a comfortable niche with their compression software which was embedded in high-end graphics cards used by gamers, scientists, engineers and designers around the world. But the market had stagnated, and new areas of work were proving hard to find. Whenever he tried to explain to Sheila what it was he did, she'd play dead, literally going limp and pretending she was unconscious.

Rami, long inured to Julian's cynical tone, was carrying on enthusiastically. 'You know how we've talked about expanding into other areas but not known how? Well, I think I may have found a path to the big money.'

'Really? You mean the three-hundred-and-sixty-degree gaming prototype using GPS?'

Rami shook his head and Julian shrugged off his disappointment. He'd spent two years developing the software that at one stage he had hoped would revolutionize online interactive gaming, but it was a dead dream. And as dreams went, Julian had come to the conclusion that it was rather pathetic.

'No, but it uses GPS technology, so you should be in your element. Tell me, what's the biggest and most recession-proof market that you can think of?'

'Drugs,' Julian said without hesitation. 'Although I can't see how drug-dealers would benefit from our expertise.' Rami stopped swivelling and leaned forward.

'Think again. Think legitimate. Think global.' Julian thought again and could only come to one unpleasant conclusion.

'The arms trade?'

'Bingo,' Rami said, pointing at Julian as if the room was full of people and he was the first to get it right. 'And the fastest-growing area of the arms trade is remote-controlled warfare using computers. No different to gaming, really. No different at all.'

Julian sat back in his chair, contemplating Rami. It was as if he was wilfully disregarding Julian's history. 'Weapons are not much better than drugs, are they?' he asked. 'Besides, you know my—'

Someone knocked on the glass door behind him. He looked round to see their office manager, Naomi, who had been with them for nearly six years. She had grown to become an indispensable part of the company and was the only woman, as far as Julian knew, that Rami looked up to, possibly because she was too old (or too black) to make it on to his sexual radar. Julian had encouraged more from Naomi who'd initially taken the secretarial job on offer as a way of filling the void caused when her kids (soon followed by their father) had flown the nest. But she'd shown an organizational ability both he and Rami lacked, acting as their de facto human resources person. If Julian hired on technical ability, Rami did it on communication skills and, if the candidate was female, looks and charm, so Naomi brought a level head and usually had a deciding vote. 'Look, we'll talk about the deal later, maybe after dinner, but I'm not talking about making weapons here, I'm talking about software. Listen,' he said, tapping Julian's knee, 'keep it under your hat for now, things could still go tits up. I haven't said anything to

Naomi.' He waved Naomi in before Julian could reply. He stood up to leave.

'By the way,' Rami said, 'can you and Sheila be at the restaurant by seven thirty tonight? We've got to eat early because Cassie's got a crack-of-dawn flight tomorrow.'

As he turned away from Rami, Julian made a face at Naomi who smiled knowingly. He went next door to his office. Rami had used the word 'deal', like he had already made one. The ache in his gut started up again but it wasn't long before he was attending to a question from one of the coders.

FOUR

S heila showered off a day's worth of London grime. She'd shown properties in central London to three interested buyers, made two valuations, taken various offers from potential buyers by phone and relayed them to sellers, then relayed back the responses. As a result she had acquired one more property for her portfolio and made exactly no sales. But some days that's how it went and she'd gained a good property to have on the books. She came out of the en suite to the sound of her ringing mobile. She checked the caller ID before she picked it up.

'Hello, Jules.'

'Hi, babe.'

'You on your way home?' She moved to face the long mirror, wedging the phone between ear and neck so she could dry herself with the towel.

'No, I'm ringing because I'm making up time for this morning at the doctor's.'

'OK. But we're meeting Rami and his new girlfriend tonight,' she said, unsure why he had to make up time since he was a partner in the company, but then he was conscientious if nothing else.

'Yep. And we have to be there by seven. She's got an early start, apparently.'

'She's probably got homework to do,' Sheila said, and listened to Julian chuckle.

'So, sell any houses today?' he asked.

'No, but I landed a brilliant one to the portfolio. A house off the Fulham Road, near South Ken Tube. They're usually divided into flats, which go for over two mil each, and this is a whole bloody house.'

'Great. I meant to ask, you're being careful, aren't you, when taking men round on their own? It's just there was that case.' Ah, yes, the case of the estate agent murdered when showing some bloke round an apartment. Sheila liked to think that her clients were a cut above that sort of thing, that rapists and murderers were priced out of the market.

'Yes, dear. I always take David with me if it's a man on his own,' she said, although she only did that after dark or if she wasn't sure about the buyer. But she wasn't going to get into a discussion with Julian about her personal safety; in some respects he was worse than her mother had been. Besides, she'd never had any trouble showing a man on his own round a house. An appreciative look, yes, and the odd invitation to dinner that she'd declined. 'Just don't be late home,' she told him.

'Well, that's the thing. Do you mind if we meet at the restaurant? You can take a taxi if you don't want to walk.'

After agreeing to see him there she hung up, turning to examine her profile in the mirror. She stood on the balls of her feet to see what effect that had on her behind. She hadn't asked Julian how he'd got on at the doctor's, but she'd lost interest in his visits and various tests about the time it had become obvious that nothing was physically wrong with him. She'd told him he should take up exercise, and suggested he join her at one of the Pilates classes she attended. But he'd called Pilates a 'women's thing' and declined, despite the promise of lithe young women in leotards to ogle. Most of them, in fact, were younger than her. She turned this way and that in front of the mirror, pulling at the skin of her neck. Not bad for someone technically nearer fifty than forty, she thought, not bad at all. Perhaps it was the silver lining to the cloud of not having had children. She stopped that train of thought by drinking from the glass of chilled white wine she'd brought up before her shower. That first drink after work was always a blessing.

Since she had the place to herself she put on Stevie Nicks'

The Other Side of the Mirror really loud, then, singing along, she danced across the polished hardwood floor to the wardrobe, from where she chose a variety of summer dresses to lay on the king-sized bed where she could contemplate them at leisure.

FIVE

I n the driver's seat of a London taxi parked on a residential street off the Parsons Green end of Fulham Road, Boris studied his dyed moustache in the rearview mirror. The taxi was rented on a weekly basis using a fake Green Badge, the licence all London cabbies needed. The tinted windows had been a pleasant bonus. In the mirror he noticed that he had missed a stray hair when trimming it that morning and took out a small penknife from which he unfolded a tiny pair of scissors. Pulling at the rogue hair, he snipped it as close to the skin as possible and checked the result. The wrinkles around his eyes he could do nothing about, but he quite liked the effect, as did the English women he paid to escort him to dinner and beyond when in London. English women were what he insisted on, none of these eastern Europeans who reminded him of those grim nights in the eighties spent doling out training to so-called allies. What a waste of time that turned out to be. He checked the mirror again. He still had a full head of thick wavy hair, and had allowed a little of the grey to remain at the temples. But the moustache couldn't be allowed to age, no way, nor could his crotch hair. He felt that there had to be consistency in an illusion, even if it was just for the benefit of women paid to enjoy his company. It was the least he could do. He found the switch that opened his window and deposited the offending hair outside. The houses were nice, semi-detached, three storeys high, bay windows on two floors, little gates on to a big enough space in the front for a couple of plant pots, sometimes a small tree. London in the summer was bearable. He could hear music playing, coming from the open window of the top floor of the house he was watching. A female vocalist, some horrible eighties

power ballad. He had come to loathe most things from the eighties. It must have been put on by the fit-looking blonde woman (even if she was a bit thin for his tastes) in the trouser suit who had arrived on foot twenty minutes ago. If this is where Julian now lived, and that woman was his wife or partner, then he had done well for himself, no doubt about that. Boris put his ear to the open window. He could swear the woman was singing along. It wasn't his type of music, really; he was more of a klezmer fan.

SIX

The first thing Julian noticed when he arrived at the restaurant on the King's Road – another bloody sushi bar that was all the fashion – was Sheila's dress. To his mind it revealed too much of her, plunging at the neck, hugging her hips and ending mid-thigh. The inappropriateness of her dress was only made more obvious by the fact that Rami's companion – late twenties, he guessed – Cassandra, who was sitting next to Sheila at a table perpendicular to the conveyor belt that circulated plates of food, had superior cleavage on display. Sheila cocked her head at him when he sat down at the table which Julian took as a 'what-about-it?' challenge, and her easy grin told him all he needed to know about how much she'd had to drink. Introductions over, they helped themselves to plates of food that passed by the table.

Cassandra was nice enough, and hardly the bimbo they had presumed she would be. She told them about her PR job in the construction industry, how she was flying to Moscow in the morning for the third time that month. Moscow was a crazy place to do business, she said. It was like someone had let the leash off capitalism.

'Have you two been to Russia at all?' she asked.

Julian shook his head.

'I spent a few months there as a teenager,' Sheila said. 'My father was at the embassy.'

Cassandra looked interested but Rami spoke first. 'Julian used to be a communist at university,' he said. 'But he saw sense in his final year. Or maybe Sheila made him see sense.'

'I wasn't really a communist as such.'

'He didn't display communist tendencies when I met him,' Sheila said. 'In fact, you were pretty anodyne when it came to politics.'

'Anodyne?' Julian said, feeling annoyed.

'I remember you attended meetings in your first year,' Rami said. Sheila looked at Julian, a question on her face.

'Well,' Cassandra was saying, 'I don't know if the Russians are better off under capitalism. Except there are some very, very rich people now and they've managed to create the illusion of democracy.'

'It's a tough one to call,' Rami said.

'No pogroms though,' Sheila said.

'That's the benchmark, is it?' Julian asked, trying to curb his annoyance. 'If there are no pogroms then everything is all right?'

'Maybe we should do business in Russia,' Rami said, picking another covered plate from the conveyor belt. They already had a small fortune of used coloured bowls stacked in the middle of the table.

'You'd love it there, Rami. It's like feminism has never happened. And some of the clubs . . . and the women, wow. But you have to be able to take your vodka.' She patted his hand, managing to be both patronizing and flirtatious. Julian could see the appeal of Cassandra to Rami. She was vivacious, pretty, articulate, a young woman in a young woman's body. In Julian's eyes there was something fake about her, but then he found himself thinking that about a lot of people he met.

'I need the loo,' Sheila said.

'I'll come with you,' Cassandra said, shuffling off the bench after Sheila, who looked surprised.

Julian smiled at Sheila; no doubt her days of going to the bathroom with other women had passed.

'You can tell me all the things about Rami he hasn't told me,' Cassandra said.

Sheila raised her eyebrows questioningly at Rami and said, 'How much to keep quiet?'

Rami smiled nervously. The women laughed and walked off, Cassandra leaning in to Sheila and chatting as they walked. Julian prodded with a chopstick at something wrapped in seaweed.

'Well, what do you think?' Rami asked. 'About Cassie, I mean.'

Julian shrugged. 'She seems nice enough.'

'There's a vote of confidence, right there.'

'Come on, man. You get through women like sushi dishes. No sooner have you chosen one than something better comes down the conveyor belt.'

He didn't say anything but fished something out of the pocket of his jacket, which was folded neatly next to him. It was a business card, which he handed to Julian.

'I took Cassie here. She loved it. Amazing little boutique hotel with a spa. Take Sheila. Treat her.'

'OK,' he said, pocketing the card unread, a little put out by being told to *treat* Sheila, like an accusation that he didn't treat her enough. He turned to Rami. 'About this deal you've concocted. I don't need to tell you I'm not getting involved in the arms trade again, even if it is on the margins. You know where I came from.'

Rami, still in his work suit, ran a hand inside his open shirt and absent-mindedly fingered the hair on his chest. It was a habit Julian used to believe betrayed self-love on Rami's part, but he now thought it to be a self-comforting thing, like when Sheila had pointed out that he unconsciously rubbed the back of his head.

'Yes. I know you came from British Aerospace and that you hated it there. I remember when you joined them straight from UCL. I was surprised given your politics, but you'd just met the lovely Sheila and you made what I thought was a pragmatic decision. Now, I want our company to make a pragmatic decision, one that will save ten jobs, possibly the business, and probably mean taking on more people.'

'Things aren't that bad, Rami. Look at the small companies that have folded.'

'Really? And we've gone from thirty people to ten because why?'

'Things fluctuate in this business, you know that. You get a contract, you take people on for the length of the contract. That's how it works in software development.'

'That's bullshit. I'm talking about a core workforce, not people we take on when we're pushed. Look, just listen to the job before you decide, it's not what you think.'

Julian could see the women coming back, single file. Cassie was in front and for a couple of seconds he appreciated the way she negotiated the chairs with her hips, like a skier on a slalom. He caught Sheila's eye and she gave him a faint smile, letting him know that she'd caught him checking Cassie out but that it was all right. He reciprocated and turned back to Rami.

'Look, I'm not doing it. Which means we're not doing it.'

'Not doing what?' Cassie said, as they got back in their seats.

'Not taking on a lucrative new contract, that's what,' Rami said. Sheila looked at Rami then Julian, but Julian gave her a this-isn't-the-time shake of the head.

'So did Sheila give you the low-down on Rami?' he asked Cassie, by way of distraction.

'It may come as a surprise to you that women don't talk about men when they are alone,' Sheila said. 'There are plenty of more interesting topics.'

'Really?' Rami asked. 'Like for instance?'

She exchanged a glance with Cassie and poured herself some more wine too quickly so that it splashed on the tablecloth.

'So what is this contract that Julian doesn't want to take on?' she said, looking directly at Rami. Julian knew she was deliberately provoking him and he was determined not to show his annoyance.

'Something that would make early retirement possible,' Rami said.

'Really? Not his silly video games thing,' she said.

'No, something using the same GPS know-how but for a more grown-up purpose. But your partner has qualms, Sheila. Principles, even.'

Sheila laughed, loud enough to turn heads at the next table.

Annoyed, Julian said to him, 'I thought we weren't supposed to talk about it?'

He shrugged. 'If it's not going to happen, it doesn't really matter now, does it?'

'I think you two guys should talk about work some other time,' Cassie said, putting her hand on Rami's. 'You're putting a downer on what was a great evening. Besides, I need to go to bed. Early start in the morning.'

Rami placed his free hand on hers. 'Then I will take you home and tuck you in,' he said.

SEVEN

With Sheila snoring lightly next to him, Julian replayed the evening's events in his head. It was irritating how an innocuous conversation, a casual question, could make him so anxious. They had decided to take the forty-minute walk home rather than hail a taxi because it wasn't yet ten o'clock and the night air was warm. Of course they'd argued, with Julian being unable to resist commenting on her choice of dress, and her calling him a repressed and hypocritical prude who was happy to ogle Cassie.

'Not that I blame you though,' she'd said. 'Do you know what it was we talked about in the toilets?'

'No.'

'You'll like this. After I'd established that she had a first in history from York we obviously discussed her breasts. She made me feel them.'

At this Julian had stopped dead on the King's Road with Sheila carrying on for a couple of steps until he said, 'She made you feel them?'

'Well, she asked me to, wanted me to. She caught me looking at them in the mirror when she was refreshing her lipstick.'

Julian had immediately known why. 'Because they're fake, right?'

She'd wagged a finger. 'Enhanced, apparently, not fake.' She'd leant against the window of a designer clothes shop and laughed without a shred of self-consciousness. He envied that about her. Envied it and hated it at the same time. Hated it because it was uncontrolled and he was wary of uncontrolled.

'What did they feel like, then? I want to know.'

'I'm sure you do.' She'd made squeezing motions with her

hands, as if to relive the experience. 'They were fantastic. Felt great. Top-of-the-range tits, she called them. That girl must make a fortune in Moscow.' She had muttered something that Julian couldn't fully make out. 'She was just a kid when the Berlin Wall fell. What does she know about communism?'

Julian had shrugged.

They'd started walking again. 'So you attended meetings at uni? What was it, Socialist Workers Party?'

'It was part of the Anti-Nazi League movement. Everyone attended SWP meetings at university,' Julian had said.

'No, they didn't. I for one felt no need. How come you never told me about it before?'

'Like Rami said, I saw sense and grew out of it. It wasn't something I was especially proud of.'

They'd walked in silence, passing Chelsea Football Club.

Sheila had shaken her head. 'She's worried about becoming thirty next year. Thirty!' She'd snorted. 'Where the hell does he find them?'

'I can't believe he actually said he was going to tuck her in.'

They'd laughed and she'd taken his arm. 'I'm proud of you for standing up to Rami about this military contract, despite your Bolshevik past,' she'd said, leaning in to him the rest of the way home, where, in the hallway, he'd helped her out of her dress, which in the privacy of their house he found incredibly sexy.

Now, since he couldn't get to sleep because of the heat, he decided on a shower to remove the cumulative stickiness of love-making and the warm night. He picked up his mobile and tiptoed to the en suite where he closed the door before putting on the light. He would have to talk to Rami properly about his mysterious lead and at least hear his proposal before dismissing it out of hand. Not that he had any intention of taking it on; it was just that he needed to at least listen properly to his partner, make time for him. He sent him a text, proposing they meet for breakfast in the morning.

Showered and back in the bedroom, he stood naked before the mirror, where in the dim light he could fool himself that he had the same body he did when thirty. The illusion became difficult to sustain when he stood sideways on.

Slipping into bed next to a gently breathing Sheila he wondered, not for the first time, whether he'd ever be able to tell her the truth about that final year at university and the years afterwards. The problem was he'd left it too long; at this stage it would do more harm than good. He could feel the familiar ache in his stomach. He decided, before he fell asleep, that he would go and see the analyst Dr Banerjee had recommended; if he couldn't talk to Sheila, and he needed to tell someone, better it was someone paid to keep secrets.

EIGHT

Julian found Rami sitting at their usual table in a café on the Caledonian Road, not two minutes' walk from the Hadfish offices. Rami had already ordered them both the full English breakfast, knowing that he'd be on time.

'Cassandra get off all right?' he asked Rami, as he swallowed some vitamin supplements with his tea.

'Yes, fine, I've come straight from the airport. She seemed to hit it off with Sheila.'

Julian nodded as if this was the expected response to such a declaration.

'What's with all the tablets?'

'They give me the illusion that I am doing something about my health. Anyway, like I said in my text, I'd like to hear more about this job of yours before I dismiss it out of hand. But I'm not promising anything.'

'That's all I ask,' Rami said, looking around him in case anyone could hear. But the place was empty apart from an old man in a flat cap nursing a mug of tea and a tabloid newspaper.

Julian caught sight of a topless model as the man unfurled his paper. Did Rami know about Cassie's implants? Sheila hadn't said if he did and he couldn't think of a way to bring up the topic. When she split up with him, which, if the past was anything to go by, Julian thought was only a matter of time, he'd be able to point it out as an obvious character flaw.

'I got talking to someone from this software company,' Rami

was saying, 'that has been contracted to produce a module of the software that is built into UAVs.' He paused and looked at Julian. 'You know, remotely operated drones. Basically it's the brains in this thing, helps it fly to the right place using GPS. Thing is this is a new UAV that's being developed, one of the biggest and with the longest range yet.'

He stopped as a young man in an apron approached with their breakfasts and plonked them on the table. Julian immediately started to saw his bacon. One of the benefits of the endless medical tests he'd had done was that he knew his cholesterol level was fine.

'Who's developing the drone?' he asked, as he layered egg on to his bacon.

'I genuinely don't know. My contact is wary of giving out details. They bid for the job and got it, probably on price, but in their tender they overplayed some of their technical strengths and now they need to fill the gaps asap.' Rami pronounced 'asap' as a word rather than an acronym, something that struck Julian as an annoying Americanism.

'Hmm, sounds familiar,' Julian said, and they smiled at a shared memory of tender submissions they had exaggerated themselves.

'What they're looking for is someone to check the set-up and see if it's robust. Make sure it passes the requirements in the tender. Since it's to do with GPS it pricked up my ears. I think they've read your paper on GPS security.'

'Have they? Well, that's probably out of date now anyway.'

The old man with the tabloid got up and left the café.

'The thing is, even if I didn't have an ethical problem with doing the job, I'd need to see the specification the tender was based on simply to be able to establish if we could, technically, do it.'

Rami had thrust a forkful of egg, bacon and mushroom into his mouth so Julian waited for him to finish.

'Yes, I can see that,' Rami said, dabbing his lips. 'Trouble is security is tight, and under the terms of their contract they'd have to get us security cleared for the subcontract. That could take weeks, and with me being Lebanese . . .'

None of this sounded right to Julian; he was used to Rami

being light on technical detail, after all it wasn't his job, but being slapdash on the contractual side was not like him. Plenty of Lebanese emigrés worked on sensitive government contracts, and besides, surely Julian's own stint at British Aerospace gave him some form, it wasn't like when he'd left there'd been any suspicion of what he'd been up to while he was there. Still, the thought of being vetted gave him stomach cramps and he was beginning to regret his breakfast.

'So you'd want us to take on this work off the books, as it were?'

'No, not entirely.' Rami leaned forward and Julian could smell his subtle aftershave. 'Look, there'll be a contract, it'll just be for something innocent. It's not unusual for companies to subcontract bits of a sensitive project without divulging the real nature of the whole project.'

'So why didn't they do that in our case? Why not just come up with a spec that didn't relate to the real purpose of the project? Why be open about it to you but not want to commit to it on paper?'

'I've explained why. It was less work this way. If they'd gone by the book they'd have to explain to their client why they needed to use another company, something they hadn't declared in their tender.'

'But no specification, no deliverables, nothing written down.'

'They're in a jam, Julian. They need us' – he gestured at Julian – 'they need you, your expertise. That's why they're willing to pay above the odds.'

Julian shook his head and mopped his plate with a crust of toast. 'I don't like it. Who is this company? What are they called?'

Rami pulled a reluctant face. 'All I know is that they're based in Leeds and that they've been involved in developing software for the military before.'

'Please don't tell me you want me to work for a client we don't even know the name of, with no written spec. Please, Rami.'

'We would obviously get some more information if we showed interest. But since you don't want to do it anyway then it doesn't really matter, does it? Let me ask you this: if I had a spec, security clearance, a proper contract, etc., would you take it on then?'

Julian sipped his tea and sat back. 'I would at least consider it, because I would know what I was dealing with.' He put his mug down and pushed his empty plate aside. 'You know what these drones do, don't you?'

'Yes, they fly over places and take surveillance photographs.'

'Don't be disingenuous, man. They're used to hit human targets. Extrajudicial killing, I think they call it.'

'You really need to stop reading the *Guardian*. So they take out a few Muslims, some al-Qaeda or Taliban scum. Big fucking deal. Who's going to miss them?'

'I don't know, their families?'

Rami was a Maronite Christian and his dislike of Muslims was nothing new to Julian. He insisted that they, along with the Palestinians, had ruined his country of origin. 'Besides, they don't just take out "bad guys", Rami, they take out women and children. A whole wedding party in Afghanistan. Remember that? You want our software in a machine that does that?'

'That's like blaming Facebook because paedophiles use it.'

'No, it's not the same thing at all. We'd be designing software for the purpose of killing. If Facebook were making software specifically for paedophiles, then we would rightly blame them, but they're not.'

'It wouldn't be our software. We'd just be testing it.'

'Come on. Is that supposed to make it OK?'

Rami sat back and sighed, showing Julian his palms in defeat. 'To be honest I thought you'd want to be involved in something more interesting than making faster and cheaper graphics cards for gaming teenagers.'

'We've done OK by it, and it's not just gamers who benefit,' Julian said, secretly agreeing that he found no pleasure in the work. It lacked purpose and direction and Sheila thought it laughable despite the fact that estate agents weren't held in the highest esteem. 'Isn't there something else in the pipeline?' he asked, trying to steer things on to more productive ground.

'Some bits and pieces, nothing major like this. Nothing that could lead to other lucrative work.' He took a breath. 'You know, Jules, I've worked hard to make our company what it is, but you do not seem to have the same investment in its future as I do.'

'Hang on a minute, Rami—'

'No, listen. If your politics are going to get in the way of business then maybe we have a problem.'

Rami was avoiding his gaze; Julian had never seen him so worked up.

'This is really an issue for you, isn't it?'

Rami looked at the heavens and held up his hands. 'Finally you take me seriously.'

'I always take you seriously,' Julian said, smiling.

'Bullshit.' He stood up and threw some money on the table. 'I'm going to the office.' He strode off without waiting for Julian, who was left studying the remains of his breakfast. He tucked the money under a plate with the bill and checked his phone for emails and messages before leaving, just to give Rami a head start.

NINE

The six-floor property (including basement) on Onslow Square was one of many in a smart line of white terraced houses. Sheila knew that a lot of these houses had been divided into flats, so she was extremely pleased with herself for landing a whole house to sell. The years of networking and being diligent at her job had paid off.

The houses had their numbers painted in black on the white pillars standing on either side of steps that formed deep Doric porches complete with coach lights. Although she loved this part of London, a lot of the buyers here were investment companies rather than people setting up home. At one time rich Arabs had snapped up properties in the area, and Rami had been a good contact in that regard, but the last few years had seen an increase in Russian buyers, who sent their kids to private schools in the UK and made an investment at the same time. She liked selling houses because she liked meeting people, even though her super-rich clients were a breed unto themselves. It was the less rarefied bit of the market that she enjoyed most, like where she lived with Jules, but even that, she knew, was out of the reach of most. After years of working for others, she now owned her own business, with one occasional employee, David, and ran a virtual office, thinking of herself more as a matching service than an estate agent; a kind of dating agency for people and houses, where they came to her with their requirements and she actively found something for them, sometimes even if it wasn't on the market. Her clients didn't go into estate agents on the high street, nor did they surf the web looking for properties. They had an area in mind, a size requirement or a type of house and occasionally, just occasionally, a price bracket.

She had done well over the years, and was proud to be financially independent of Julian. She'd heard many of her friends pontificating about feminism, or relying on their husband's income to pursue a hobby dressed up as a business. But for her this was what it boiled down to: having the ability to survive economically on your own. She'd had this drilled into her by her mother, a woman trapped in a loveless marriage with a husband who was moderately successful as a minor diplomat. She'd accepted material things from him, the value of which were inversely proportional to the attention he paid her, so she'd told Sheila after her father's death, confiding that she'd resorted to seeking physical affection elsewhere. Cassie, she felt, understood this, despite the boob job. She clearly worked hard. Maybe the boobs were just her way of gaming what was a male-orientated system, turning what was expected of her to her advantage. No, until a woman achieved financial independence, any pretensions of being a feminist were just that. Sheila had even put enough money away in the hope that when she and Jules had children, she would not be dependent on him for the period she chose to be off work, and would be able to pay for childcare herself. But the children hadn't happened. He'd never been keen. There existed a side to Jules he held back, something unrevealed she couldn't put her finger on. It was a straitjacket, whatever it was, that kept him from being himself. He was scared of showing any vulnerability, like last night's silly business with the dress she was wearing, and the fact that he'd kept his politics at university quiet. He hadn't minded the dress when they'd got home, quite the opposite.

She unlocked the gloss-black door using keys from a carefully numbered bunch and stepped into the empty house. Jules was afflicted with fear, she thought. Fear of what, she wasn't sure, but there had been several points in their relationship, especially when he'd been at British Aerospace, when she'd wondered if he was seeing someone from work. Sexual betrayal was something one half-expected in men, after all, but to her mind a much worse crime was his confiding in another woman. For him to whisper his deepest fears to another didn't bear thinking about. Ironically, all this had driven her, she believed, to an indiscretion of her own, one that made her cringe when she thought of it now. It was after that lapse of judgement that she'd stopped mentioning children. And now, of course, it was too late.

Standing inside the front door she took a moment to savour the feeling. This was a part of the job she loved, being alone in empty houses and apartments, the creak of the uncovered floor-boards, the echo of her footfalls. It evoked new beginnings and possibilities. This house was huge; she was looking forward to going through it properly on her own. First things first: she found the downstairs bathroom and sat on the toilet with the door wide open, her view down the hall to the front door unimpeded. The sound of her urine splashing against the enamel sounded pleas-ingly loud in the empty space. She looked round to see no toilet paper but she always carried tissues in her bag, knowing from experience that the rich often took these small things with them when they moved house. Sometimes even the light bulbs were gone. She washed her hands and had a pleasant recollection of last night's sex. That was when Jules seemed most able to be himself, during sex. It was like opening a door into a hidden room. He became direct, responsive and confident. Masterful, even, although she would never tell him that. She smiled at her reflection, holding it rictus-like to study the resulting wrinkles. Laughter wrinkles, Jules called them, bless him, yet she knew he could see her ageing, just as she could. Some things were made harder for a woman.

'You're fucking amazing,' she said loudly to her reflection, repeating what he had said to her last night. Not straight after relaxing on to her back, she happily taking his weight, him still panting in her ear. Not even as they lay on their backs, her head on his damp chest, his hand resting in the small of her back. But later, as he came out of the shower smelling of sandalwood, and she was passing him naked to use the shower herself. He'd grabbed her and said it then, and she'd felt like a teenager again.

Singing loudly, she went round the house with a rubbish bag and inspected cupboards and drawers: in the kitchen (nothing), built-in wardrobes upstairs (a lonely shoe with a broken heel), cabinets in the three bathrooms (an empty bottle of conditioner for blonde hair). She also took measurements of the rooms and photos using her smartphone.

She checked the time: when she was done here she'd walk to the Chelsea and Westminster Hospital on the Fulham Road, where she had an appointment. She'd been volunteering there one afternoon a week for over a year, something she kept from Jules because she could hear his cynical scoff, telling her that she was just soothing her liberal guilt. Perhaps he thought it best, like him, to do nothing. But volunteering at the hospital had not just given her a sense of satisfaction, it had also presented an opportunity to put some of her savings and time to even better use, which was what she was going to explore at her lunchtime meeting.

TEN

B oris sat in the back of his taxi across from the building where Hadfish Systems rented office space. It was on York Way, just a few minutes' walk from King's Cross station, and a nightmare for parking; he'd been lucky to find his spot on a side street running past the building – it had its own underground parking that he couldn't access – and he'd already received a parking ticket. From his vantage point he could just about see the car-park entrance. He had established his own office in the back of his taxi, hidden from passers-by thanks to the tinted windows.

He'd been there for over an hour, having come from watching Julian's partner, Sheila (today dressed in jeans and T-shirt), let herself into a large residential house on an upmarket square in

Kensington. He loved Kensington, but it had been bought up as investment by the very Russians he despised, and lots of it remained empty most of the time since they didn't live there.

He'd established, over the last two days, using his 3G-connected tablet and a few phone calls, that (a) Sheila and Julian were not married, and (b) she ran her own agency selling property, which explained the visit to the house in Kensington where he'd left her. He'd also realized that she must be the same Sheila Dove that he'd had checked out in 1980. Her father, as he recalled the records showing, had been a small-time British diplomat, some minor trade functionary, which had naturally generated some interest in the KGB, especially as he'd spent a few months stationed in the Soviet Union just as Reagan's ridiculously strict technology embargo had kicked in. However, it had emerged that he was clean, a nobody. He'd watched Julian and Sheila leave their house together earlier that morning, Julian by car and Sheila on foot. They'd had a brief conversation before parting, one where she'd tried to make eye contact but he was already elsewhere, focused on something yet to happen. No hug or kiss, unless they'd done that inside the house.

That's when he'd decided to follow Sheila rather than Julian, who he knew was going to the office anyway. She wasn't critical to the matter in hand, but he felt it prudent at this stage to keep all angles covered, and you never knew what information, however innocuous, would come in useful later.

'I wouldn't mind covering her angles,' he said aloud, chuckling to himself. OK, so maybe she wasn't his type, he gravitated more towards the hourglass figure, but to be honest about it, he enjoyed following her around. It gave him a buzz. When he'd seen her being picked up by taxi last night he'd wished he'd known that she'd ordered one, because he might have risked picking her up in his taxi, such was his high-spirited mood.

It made him reckless, being in London. It was such a change from Azerbaijan; what a shit posting that had turned out to be. They only had themselves to blame, of course, fucking relations up with Turkey like that, but it had provided an opportunity to be physically closer to the enemy. But Baku was such a dull city, and no English women to speak of unless you counted the slim pickings among the expatriate community. So being transferred to London – thanks to his experience here – at this time of year, was even better than being back in Beersheba, a desert city in the country that he now called home, where the temperature would currently be unbearably high.

His phone rang and it took a few seconds to realize it was the encrypted satellite phone, not his mobile. Ears in Baku must be burning, he thought.

'Hello?' he said.

'Hello, comrade Borya,' a male voice said in Russian, after a crackly delay.

Boris smiled at the salutation.

'Have you made any progress?'

'Yes, contact has been made,' Boris said, also in Russian. 'But it looks like I may have to use more persuasion. I am just confirming this as we speak.'

'OK, do whatever you have to do, to move things along.'

'Problems?'

'You mean apart from the one you are dealing with? Yes, our friends from the East are becoming more assertive, so stay awake. I'll contact you when I know more.'

'OK. Goodbye, comrade.'

He snapped open a can of Coke, sipping at it while considering how to proceed. He might have to resort to showing his hand with Julian, it was just a matter of how he did it. His superiors considered his trip to London to be an unwelcome development, hence the snide reference to it in the phone call. After all, it was he who had recommended using the company in Leeds that now said they didn't have the technical know-how to do the job they'd originally said they could. But being unpopular was a small sacrifice to make in the scheme of things. Boris had never cared about being popular, even at the cost of not belonging. He'd briefly hoped he might find somewhere to belong when he'd moved to Israel. Now he felt that in his desperation to escape the uncomfortable reality of a post-Soviet Russia to which he could not reconcile himself, he'd landed somewhere worse: a self-imposed prison whose walls were indeterminable, where he was looked on by the sabra as an outsider, and regarded suspiciously by the older refusenik Russians who had arrived during perestroika. He got the sense that they knew what he had been back in Russia. Unlike them he had arrived with a job.

He took the leather-bound journal from the seat beside him, removed the large elastic band that kept it together, and opened to a blank page. 'Three walls' he wrote, then divided the page into three and wrote a), b) and c) beneath the lines. He tapped his pen against his chin, thinking. He had spent a lot of time thinking, and there came a time when you have to act, to make a choice about the sort of world you wanted to live in.

As for 'our friends from the East', they may be able to operate in Azerbaijan easily, but they were hamstrung over here since they'd stopped killing exiles in the West and Western intelligence agencies now had Muslims firmly in their sights.

No, he wasn't worried about them at all. He just hoped they were the right kind.

His eyelids started to droop and he thought about reclining on the back seat to catch up on his sleep, but was startled by his phone ringing again. This time it was his mobile. The call he'd been waiting for.

'Shalom,' he said into the phone, crushing the empty can using only his fingers.

ELEVEN

In her three-star hotel bedroom somewhere in north London, Mojgan woke after a ten-hour sleep, her mouth dry. She gulped bottled water, showered and washed her long black hair, which always took a long time. Farsheed loved her hair, but complained about how long it took her to look after it, and about the hairs he found in the shower, or in the bed, or sometimes even in the food.

'You can't have the one without the other. Do you want me to cut it off?'

No, he didn't.

Sitting on the bed wrapped in a large towel, another around her head, she opened the parcel she had picked up the night

before from the address she'd memorized. It had turned out, after
a long and expensive taxi ride, to be a family residence where
they had a painting in the hall showing the Battle of Karbalā of
61AH. The woman of the house had been keen to give Mojgan
her parcel and see the back of her.

There were three separate packets inside the parcel. One was
a cellophane-wrapped box, a key-logger. She opened it and
removed the logger from its plastic cover. This particular one
(she'd seen many) looked like a USB stick but with a connection at each end; one plugged into the computer, the other into
the keyboard cable. She could have bought it herself from any
decent computer shop but Farsheed had ordered it for her
because he wanted to make sure she had the right type, nothing
wireless or that could be detected once installed. The key-logger
recorded each and every keypress made on the keyboard it was
connected to, and could store millions of keystrokes. Its advantage was that no amount of software protection, be it firewalls,
spyware detection or hard-disk cryptography, could guard
against it. And since that's where most people's attention was
focused in terms of computer security, it was a beautifully
uncomplicated solution to discovering what was keyed into
someone's computer, and what they were doing online, including
account details and passwords. Of course, it could not access
anything on the hard drive prior to its installation but its biggest
disadvantage was obvious: since it needed to be connected
between the keyboard and the computer, she would need physical access to the target computer to both fit it and, when it had
captured enough data, retrieve it, even if it was just for several
seconds. This, then, would be her first challenge: gaining access
to the premises, once she knew where it was.

The second, smaller item in the parcel was a heavily taped
envelope that contained eight SIM cards preloaded with credit.
They had numbers written on them, one to eight.

The third and heaviest packet was wrapped in brown paper
and a lot of brown packing tape. She had to use her nail scissors
to cut it open and when she did she laid it on the bed in disbelief:
a small handgun. If she made the shape of a gun with her thumb
and forefinger it was shorter even than that. It had *Ruger* etched
just above the grip. She picked it up. It weighed nothing and

seemed tailor-made for her small hand. On the other side, where the cartridges were expelled, it said *380 Auto*. She was no fire-arms expert but she and Farsheed had gone shooting together a few times at the ministry practice range outside Tehran. This was lighter and smaller than any of the heavy handguns she had handled there. She figured out how to eject the magazine and found it had six rounds in it. She clicked it back in and made sure the safety was on before sticking it in the bottom of her handbag. Why had he provided it? He'd not suggested that she'd need a weapon, nothing suggested that the mission would be dangerous. Why hadn't he mentioned it?

She thought about this as she finished drying her hair using the hairdryer in the bathroom, then tied it and pinned it up using eighteen hairpins. She might be OK with the idea that she wouldn't be wearing a scarf in public, but she only let her hair down for one man.

She had once been stopped by the so-called morality police outside the entrance to Tehran University, two women in black chadors who were clearly from some backward village in the west of Iran, recruited for their ignorance and bad skin. They had something to say about her hijab; it either hadn't covered her hair and neck enough or it was too colourful, she couldn't remember. At the time she had been working for the Ministry of Intelligence and National Security and had thrown them by flashing her badge and telling them she was on official business, which was true. After consulting with their male superior, he came up to her and insisted on seeing her badge. She showed it to him but refused to hand it over, instead taking out a note-book and pen, demanding his name and police number. He had scurried off, like the flea-ridden dog he was. She was, therefore, spared a trip to the station in the minibus (already filled with code-flouting women) where they would all have received a lecture on how to dress properly.

She placed the logger and SIM cards in a small zippered compartment in her bag, then stuffed in the packaging. She wondered whether it would be better to leave the weapon in the room or take it with her. She decided to keep it with her and to change hotels. Dressed in her suit she went down for breakfast, avoiding the several types of cooked meat on offer at the buffet and sticking to cereal and yoghurt. She ate without much joy and quickly, just another person on business keen to get on. She disposed of the packaging from her bag in a bin outside the hotel before finding a taxi.

It was only as she was well on her way to Tottenham Court Road – somewhere that hotel reception had advised her contained many computer shops – that she switched on her phone and logged into the word game app to check the status of yesterday's game. She swore under her breath; he had put in another long word. He was definitely cheating, probably using one of those anagram-solving websites and putting in the letters he had.

There was a private message. *Did you do your shopping?*

Yes. I have found everything I need, plus more, she typed, hoping he would get her reference. She studied the letters she had and placed a word on the virtual board. He was still winning. It wasn't long until he responded; he must have been waiting up for her, attuned to her time zone.

Anything extra may be useful, he typed.

I hope I did not waste money on unnecessary things, she typed, pushing him for a bit more information. She waited, looking out as the taxi crawled along in traffic. No one, she noticed, used their horns here. Eventually a message came back.

You never know when you will need it. This was not very reassuring.

She stared out at the drab streets and wondered if she'd get a chance to see any tourist attractions. Probably not, but if she could make a little time to do some shopping for herself she'd be pleased, and she had also promised to pick up something more vital for her neighbour. Some medicines were now in short supply in Iran, not because they were on the sanctions list, but because banks in the West were loath to take money from Iranian institutions in case they fell foul of the sanctions. Farsheed's own mother had run out of Herceptin for her breast cancer, and it was only due to her son's connections that they'd been able to source some from a businessman who'd stockpiled it before it had become difficult to import into the country. Farsheed had told her that there was an Iranian producer who was set up and licensed to make the product, but the official who signed off on production was related to the same businessman he had sourced his from. It was stories like this that upset Mojgan, and she was ashamed that they had benefited from this when others couldn't. Not to mention the officials who came to London for treatment when their countrymen made do. But it was Farsheed's mother they were talking about, and that was the only reason she hadn't tackled him too strongly about it, even though usually she wasn't shy about voicing her displeasure at injustices. She knew she took it too far sometimes, not because she was wrong, but because the consequences of being too vocal could be damaging to her and Farsheed's careers. They may have managed to sort his mother out with drugs, but her neighbour was another matter, and Mojgan felt guilty enough that she was willing to take the time out on this trip to do it.

The driver let her out near the top of Tottenham Court Road and she went shopping for a small laptop or netbook and a USB to PS/2 converter. Farsheed might have bought the correct key-logger, but he had not considered the possibility that she might be faced with an older-style keyboard that had a round plug. This is why they made such a good team. Her phone buzzed.

I will finish this game tomorrow. I have to go and work.

She switched the phone off. That night she would start down-loading all the software she needed from a server Farsheed would temporarily make available.

TWELVE

After his run-in with Rami (he didn't know what else to call it), Julian had gone back to the office, only to find he'd already left. Naomi was clueless about where he was but was itching to hear about the new girlfriend.

'So, is she pretty?' she asked, bringing in his post and some papers.

'What do you think?'

'I think she's pretty and curvaceous. He likes them curvaceous.'

Julian nodded, taking his post.

She held on to the papers. 'And young?'

'Of course. She might be the youngest yet.'

'Why do men, as they get older, like their women ever younger?' she said, not without bitterness.

Julian shrugged. 'To negate the fact that we're getting old?'

She smiled. He liked her smile; she always had one at the ready, but he sometimes detected a sadness in it, a secret, or a regret. He'd sometimes wondered what it was like for her, starting over again. It wasn't the same for women, Sheila had said when they'd once discussed Naomi, not when they got older. Naomi never mentioned anyone special or plans for the weekend. He thought she might have a cat. He had been tempted to give her a hug, once or twice, but whether this was because she gave off some maternal quality and *he* needed the hug or because he felt sorry for her, he wasn't sure. Neither was really a good reason to jeopardize an excellent working relationship. He'd driven her to her flat in Bloomsbury once, after one of the company outings Rami insisted on, bowling or something, and she'd invited him in. There were framed pictures of her boys on display, with young kids of their own. He'd accepted a herbal tea and sunk into her sofa and listened to some classical radio she put on. Yes, there had been a cat, he remembered now. He'd felt oddly at home there, and would have gladly spilled all his secrets to her given the slightest encouragement. He'd left as soon as he'd finished his tea, and she'd brushed his cheek with her fingers at the door when saying goodbye. She'd smelled of grown-up perfume and gin.

He always made sure she got flowers or chocolates when she'd worked overtime to help get a tender submitted. He always told her that they were from both him and Rami, but he knew that she knew they were his doing.

Naomi went to the door and Julian thought she was leaving but she came back, standing before his desk like someone needing to make a confession. She probably wanted to gossip a bit more – not her most appealing trait. He launched the email program on his laptop to make it known he needed to work.

'Sorry, I just wondered if you'd mind signing off the expenses for last month.' She was holding a folder which she proffered tentatively.

'Rami usually does that, doesn't he?'

'Yes, but he's been out a lot and they're overdue at the accountants.'

'Can you leave them with me?'

She shifted on her feet. 'Normally I would but I really need to get them off.'

Julian took the folder and opened it. It was a list of payments on the credit cards that he and Rami, as directors, had. They were linked to an expenses account they used when travelling or entertaining clients. Although they paid an accounting firm to do all their finance, Rami and Julian gave all the receipts to Naomi for processing and Rami just signed them off.

'I'm assuming the receipts match the statement? I'm not supposed to check them, am I?' This sort of administrative thing bored him.

'Yes, all the card payments match. There are a couple of cash withdrawals that don't have receipts, but that's all.'

'I don't understand.'

'I mean Rami took some cash out on his card but there are no receipts to show what he spent the money on.' She looked uncomfortable talking about it, he noticed, as if she didn't want to cast aspersions on Rami.

'So have you spoken to Rami? He's the one who racks up the hotels and mileage.'

She pulled a face that indicated a difficulty with this approach. 'Yes, of course, but he's difficult to pin down and I don't have to explain how shoddy his record keeping is.'

'No, you don't.'

She reached out for the papers but he flipped through the statement to pick out the cash withdrawals.

'I've never used the card to withdraw cash; they charge you. Besides, we have petty cash for stuff like that.'

'They were all done on Rami's card,' she said quickly.

He went through it, mentally totting up the cash withdrawals in his head: £500 in Leeds, nearly £3,000 in London. This was a lot of money to take out in cash. Fifty quid here and there he could understand, but £3,500? Rami had mentioned Leeds only that morning, although in another context.

'Did you say you'd spoken to Rami about this?'

'Sort of – I don't think he's got the receipts. It doesn't really matter, except the accountancy firm will query it.'

He nodded. 'I'm sure there's an innocent explanation. Don't worry, I'll take care of it.'

'You're not going to sign them off?'

'Well, no, I'll need to speak to Rami first. Sorry.' She looked unhappy as she left the office, as if he'd interfered in her process. But she had come to him, and he wasn't as lackadaisical as Rami was about this stuff, not when it came to this amount of money in difficult times. What the fuck was Rami up to? He'd have to tackle him when he reappeared, but given their conversation that morning he wasn't looking forward to it. It was possible that his card had been cloned or something. Yes, that would explain it, but he thought it safer to check with Rami before cancelling the card.

With Naomi gone he closed the door and put the statement away. From his wallet he retrieved the piece of paper given to him by Dr Banerjee. Taking a deep breath he dialled the number.

'Hello?' a woman said.

'I'm ringing to make an appointment with Doctor Truby.'

'This is Doctor Truby. Is this your first visit?'

'Erm, yes,' Julian said, taken aback that she had answered herself; he was expecting a secretary. 'Doctor Banerjee said I might . . . sort of benefit from seeing you.'

'Doctor Banerjee?' You didn't hear it very often any more but she had the voice of a heavy smoker.

'Yes, in Harley Street?'

'Harley Street,' she repeated, as if this were an unfamiliar place to her. 'And how did Doctor Banerjee think I could help you?'

'Well . . .' Julian wasn't expecting to have to explain himself over the phone. Nizar, one of the new coders, was hovering outside his office, waiting for him to finish. 'He seems to think I'm a hypochondriac,' Julian whispered.

'Sorry, I didn't catch that – did you say hypochondriac?'

'Yes.'

'Hmm. He actually used that word, did he?'

'No, I think he used the word psychosomatic. Perhaps we could meet and—'

'I can see you next Monday afternoon for a chat, if that suits?'

Julian gave her his details and hung up. The receiver was slippery with sweat and he had to wipe his face with a handkerchief before waving Nizar in.

By the end of the day Rami hadn't reappeared at the office and Julian had been busy with Nizar going over the the latest iteration of software for a new graphics card. Nizar had been with them just three weeks, replacing a Ukrainian kid who had failed to renew his work permit. Nizar had, as hoped, proved a more reliable team player as well as having an excellent technical background. Julian had taken him on (despite Rami's ambivalence) because of his attitude, and the fact that he had run a small software team up in Birmingham, albeit on some less technically demanding project than Hadfish usually took on. He was coming up to speed quickly though, despite needing a lot of supervision from Julian. But it was satisfying to work with a young person who was keen to stretch themselves.

Naomi popped her head round the door at five thirty and said she was going home.

'Has Rami checked in?' Julian asked her.

She shook her head. 'I keep saying you both should at least let me know where you're going, you know . . .'

'Yes, I know.'

She smiled. 'Don't stay too late – it's a gorgeous evening.'

Once the office was empty Julian shut down his computer, put on his jacket and went next door into Rami's office. His computer was off and as ever his desk was clear.

'I hope you're drumming up business somewhere and not sulking,' he said to the empty chair.

He locked both his and Rami's offices before making sure all the computers were either switched off or, if they were running processes, password protected. You could never be too careful, what with all the commercially sensitive software they worked on. The cleaners came at night and anyone could walk in. He turned off the lights and locked the door before taking the lift down to the basement car park.

As he approached his BMW, remote key at the ready, he noticed someone leaning against the hood. Julian prepared himself to get proprietorial about his car with the heavy-set moustachioed older man with a full head of hair. His head was bowed as he cleaned under his nails with a small penknife which he put away as Julian approached.

He looked up and Julian froze, his heart lurching, then settling into rapid beats. His primal instinct was to turn and run. To leave the car, his company, Sheila, everything. Just run. The man smiled and got up from the hood, brushing the trouser seat of his linen suit.

'Hello, Julian,' he said in that familiar booming voice, approaching, smiling, his hand outstretched. 'How good to see you again, *tovarisch*.'

THIRTEEN

'You mean you haven't told your husband?' Gulnar asked Sheila. They were sitting in a coffee chain in the large atrium of the Chelsea and Westminster Hospital drinking oversized coffees. Gulnar had the faded brown look common to people of mixed race.

'He's not my husband, I just live with him. We share a house.'

'OK, whatever, but don't you think he should be in the loop before you get started?' Gulnar was dressed in jeans despite the heat. 'I imagine the amount of paperwork just to get the charity up and running will be ridiculous.'

'I suppose I was waiting for it to be real before I spring it on him. Don't worry, I'll deal with the admin side. Your job will be to tell me what you need. Plus speak to sponsors, of course – we'll both have to do a fair bit of fundraising.'

'Of course, we'll need a PowerPoint presentation we can use, and I'm doing a weekend filmmaking course so we can make a film in Afghanistan.'

Sheila nodded. She was thinking about trustees, about money, about telling Jules. This thing was looking real, no longer an idea. 'Your spouse already knows what your plans are then?' Sheila asked.

'Well, of course she does. I mean, I've already been out there a couple of times so it's not like it's a bolt out of the blue to her. Plus I've been coordinating with the kids that come over to the UK.'

I haven't even told Julian that I come here to the hospital, Sheila thought. What would Gulnar think of that? What the hell is wrong with us? Did she say 'she'?

'So when will you come out?' Gulnar asked.

Had Sheila missed something? 'Come out where?'

'To Afghanistan, of course, silly. You'll need to see things first hand. You'll need to see the kids, won't you? Cheeky rascals, most of them, although a lot are pretty traumatized.' Gulnar was peering at her through her long, mascara-free eyelashes.

'To be honest with you,' said Sheila. 'I hadn't even thought about it.'

'Really?' Gulnar said. 'It's perfectly safe, if you're careful.' She put her hand on Sheila's knee. 'You'll love it. I'll look after you, don't worry.'

'I'm not worried about it.' Although she was filled with apprehension about the whole endeavour.

'Is it the cost? Because we can raise some money . . .'

Sheila shook her head. She'd envisioned something she could do from the safety of her home office, perhaps sipping wine as she composed begging emails. 'And your partner doesn't mind you going out there?' she asked Gulnar.

'I have distant family in Kabul, so she couldn't really object. Although between you and me I've all but stopped seeing them when I go out, since they keep trying to marry me off to a Kabul lawyer or doctor. Who knows what they'd do if they knew I was living with a woman.'

Sheila looked at Gulnar afresh with this confirmation about her sexual orientation; she couldn't help it.

'I thought I'd get that out of the way early on, you know, since we're going to be working together.'

'You mean about you needing to be married off?'

Gulnar laughed. 'Nice one.'

They talked more details, with Sheila taking notes. Gulnar started talking about a suitable celebrity they could get to be a patron, even though they had yet to produce something called a governing document, never mind register the charity.

'Jude Law – do you think he'd do it?' Gulnar asked Sheila.

'Is he the right person?' Sheila countered. She didn't really know Gulnar well enough, or maybe it was a cultural thing, but she couldn't tell if she was pulling her leg.

'Probably not, but he'd look good in a promo film. Think of the fun we'd have making a film with him.'

Sheila raised her eyebrows at Gulnar. 'You fancy Jude Law?'

'Just because I'm living with a woman doesn't mean I can't appreciate a good-looking man.'

'We're probably getting a little ahead of ourselves,' Sheila said, gathering up the leaflets and guidance she had only just received from the Charity Commission. 'But maybe a woman would suit our needs better.'

A lot of work needed doing to get this off the ground. If she could just shift the Onslow Square house she'd be able to take some time out to deal with all this initial paperwork, perhaps, and, why not, go out to Afghanistan. She'd travelled abroad a lot as a kid, her father having been in the diplomatic service, but that was mainly in Europe.

'Let's do dinner at some point, with our spouses,' Gulnar said. 'Bring them up to speed.'

They parted company and Sheila walked home slowly so that when she got there it wouldn't be too obscenely early to pour some wine. She'd need a couple of glasses before she told Julian what she'd got herself into.

FOURTEEN

'Are you Jewish?' Boris asked Julian.

'What?' They were sitting in the back of Julian's BMW, not somewhere Julian had ever sat before, but Boris had insisted. Julian was having trouble breathing, and it wasn't just due to Boris's overpowering aftershave. He tried to crack open a window but since the car key wasn't in the ignition he couldn't activate the electric switch. To ameliorate his discomfort and mask his fear he decided to concentrate on how Boris had changed. His stomach, like Julian's, had expanded, but even more; it was testing the stitching on his shirt buttons. Unlike Julian he had retained his hair, which had greyed at the temples, and he'd grown a moustache. He still had that inane grin that belied his profession.

'There used to be a small nature reserve near here, opened in the mid-eighties,' Boris was saying. 'I used it for dead-letter drops and the occasional meeting for a while. It's just round the corner. Have you been?'

Julian shook his head. Naomi had mentioned somewhere she occasionally took her packed lunch, and had once suggested that he join her to counter the effects of being deskbound.

'Do you remember the drops we used at Highgate Cemetery? You wouldn't believe how many spooks from the embassy used Highgate Cemetery. We'd compete to see how close to Marx's tomb we could get our drops.' He chortled, revealing the yellow teeth of a smoker, although he seemed to have lost the smell of stale cigarettes that Julian used to associate with him. 'I bet, comrade, that if we went there right now, I could point out every dead-letter drop I used.'

Julian wished he still smoked, so he had something to do instead of speak, which he seemed incapable of doing. He did remember the nooks and crannies he stuffed his microfilm into. Every single one of them, but he wasn't about to engage in a nostalgic recollection of spy tradecraft with this man.

'So, Julian, are you a Jewish boy? I mean, with your name and everything?'

'My name?'

'Yes. Julian Fisher.'

'My father's family were German originally. It used to be spelt with a "c",' he said, although he wasn't sure why he was bothering to humour Boris, except that he might get this over with, whatever this was.

'And your mother? She's the one who's key here. I can't remember her surname.'

'Her surname was Humphreys. As far as I know she wasn't Jewish. She was Welsh.'

Boris looked disappointed.

'What's this all about?' Julian pressed.

'I'm a Jew,' Boris said. 'Did you know that?'

'How would I know that? I don't even know your last name.'

'Reznik. It's Reznik. They were never keen on Jews in KGB Moscow, not rising to the top, anyway. I'm a Jew but I'm only now trying to be Jewish. They're two different things. Back then, even though I didn't know what it meant, I was held back because of it, sent to the Eastern bloc.'

'Really? Are you sure it wasn't because you were too high-spirited?'

Boris turned to contemplate him and Julian tried to hold his nerve, but he was sweating despite the coolness of the underground car park. 'What's your view on Iran?'

'What the hell are you on about?'

'I thought we could catch up on politics. Have you stopped following what goes on in the world?'

Julian turned to Boris. 'Just cut to the fucking chase, Boris.'

Boris put his big hands up. 'OK, OK. Have it your way. I thought we could do this amicably, from a common ideological platform, but it appears not.' He took a breath. 'We have a history, you and I, don't we?'

'Yes, but it is history. It was a long time ago, Boris, and I've moved on.'

'I see that, yes. You've done very well, Julian. Nice software company, nice house, a nice woman – in fact, the same one I vetted all those years ago. I admire that kind of devotion and loyalty. But no children? And you didn't marry?'

Julian kept himself from reacting; he knew that was what Boris wanted.

'The thing is, comrade, none of what you have now would have been possible without me, without the help of the Union of Soviet Socialist Republics. You would never have got a foothold at British Aerospace, would you? And you would never have been able to start your own company without those years of experience.' Boris was drilling into Julian with his dark eyes, his tone less jovial. Julian looked longingly at the rectangle of daylight at the bottom of the slope that led to the car park exit and the street.

With great effort, he turned to Boris. 'That was a long time ago. Besides, I think I've already paid my dues.'

Boris took hold of the headrest in front of him with both hands.

His hands were large and hairy, his fingers like bristled chipolatas. 'Yes, you were an excellent investment and provided great returns.' He seemed to be addressing the headrest, his knuckles whitening and his thumbs sinking into the leather. 'Does Sheila know what you used to do? Does your business partner, your employees? Do the people you have contracts with? Your neighbours? The people you invite round to your dinner parties, the people you call your friends?'

Julian's sweat turned cold and Boris turned to smile at him, releasing his grip on the headrest, then checking his fingernails. They looked suspiciously like they'd been professionally manicured to Julian, who was unable to speak.

'No, I thought not. A secret like that has consequences, doesn't it, if it comes out? Like ripples in a pond, or in your case, a tsunami. A tsunami of truth,' he said, clearly pleased with his analogy.

All Julian could do was shake his head, which released drops of sweat on to his trousers.

'And, of course, if the authorities were to learn of your treachery, who knows what investigations they would need to carry out?'

'After all this time?' Julian said, finding his voice. 'None, I imagine. They've got other things to worry about.'

'Maybe you're right. They have let other traitors retire gracefully, that's true, to spare themselves the embarrassment, but usually academics and journalists, low-grade spies, not those involved in passing multiple technical secrets during a strict technology embargo. And besides, if they were led to believe you were still active in some way, with the same masters but with a different ideology . . . ?' He shook his head, saying, almost to himself, 'How easily they all managed to change their beliefs, those fair-weather communists.'

Again with the cold sweat; it ran between his shoulder blades. 'What do you want, Boris?'

Boris showed his yellow teeth and gently patted Julian's right knee. 'Ah! Now we are getting somewhere. What does Boris want? How do we keep Boris happy?' Two suited men carrying briefcases walked past the front of the car, oblivious to him and Boris. Boris watched them and turned back to Julian. 'All I need, Julian,' he said, 'is for you to do your job and get well rewarded for it. That is all. Is that such a hardship?'

Julian shrugged, studying Boris warily. It crossed his mind to offer Boris money to go away, but he'd read that a lot of ex-KGB officers had done very well for themselves in the new Russia. 'You're offering me a job?'

'Not you, your company. And I'm not offering it – you've already been offered it. You just need to say yes.'

It took Julian a full minute to realize what Boris was on about. 'You approached Rami?'

Boris shook his head. 'No. I've never met him.' He mulled something over. 'Let us just say, comrade, that I have a financial interest in the company that did approach him, and that I'm keen for you to help them. Let's say that. I need to think of my retirement, Julian, as should you.' He tried to find the door handle. 'I'm not an unreasonable person. Think it over. Go home to your lovely house, in your lovely car, to your lovely woman. Be certain to make love to her tonight and as you do, as you are looking down at her – or up at her, if that's what she prefers – ask yourself whether it is all worth hanging on to.' He managed to open the door and the courtesy light came on. Before he got out Julian could see that Boris's moustache was uniformly black and overly shiny. He stuck his head back in the car. 'Tomorrow, let's say.' He paused and gave a half-smile. 'For the sake of drama, by noon, I would like to hear from the people that approached you that Hadfish Systems has accepted the job. Once that happens, I'll be in touch with the details. If not . . .'

He removed his head and closed the door. Julian watched him walk up the slope into the light and sat there for several minutes, his gut in knots, before getting into the driver's seat.

FIFTEEN

The doctor was sweating, despite his office being air-conditioned. Mojgan sat facing him, one buttock on the desk to give herself a height advantage, and waited. There was an examination table in the corner, a small sink and a

lightbox on the wall which she assumed was to study X-rays. The doctor was balding and very thin.

'Twelve months?' he asked in Farsi.

'Yes,' she said. She'd found his name on a spreadsheet back in Tehran; known exiles abroad who had spoken out against the Republic in one form or another, either online or in print. She'd sorted the list by profession and hit upon this man in the group of doctors. A cancer specialist. He had family back in Tehran – an ageing father with health problems.

'I don't have to tell you that of course I disagree with many of the sanctions,' he was saying, attempting, by way of a smile, to resurrect some of the oily charm he'd first displayed when she'd arrived at his private clinic on Harley Street pretending to be a patient. 'They have placed an intolerable burden in terms of banking and the transfer of money back home.' Realizing that he was complaining about his own financial situation, he tried a more professional air, moving on to a safer topic. 'I should, of course, examine the patient and at least see her medical notes, but given the circumstances . . .'

'So, a twelve-month course of Herceptin – can you get it for me?'

'Yes, yes. To be taken every three weeks. Can she get it infused?'

'We have hospitals and doctors in Iran, just no medicine,' she said, trying to keep her voice from going shrill.

He reddened and nodded. 'Of course, of course. I will get it for you, in concentrated powder form. It will be easier to transport. Can you come next week?'

'I'll come in two days.'

'Of course, two days.'

She stood up and walked to the door, thinking that he might try to be a man between now and when they next met. She turned to say,'Your father has a nice flat in central Tehran, does he not? He gets a pension, healthcare. He wants for nothing?'

'Yes, yes he does, praise be to God. No complaints.'

'Good, then let there be no more complaints. This will put you in a good light, what you are doing. I'll see you the day after tomorrow.'

*   *   *

Outside, on Harley Street, feeling, as she always did after such an encounter, a little nauseated, she stood to take her bearings. She could have used her phone to locate herself but she had disabled the GPS facility on it. Oxford Street was somewhere near here, but which direction? She would like to buy some more comfortable shoes, she was doing a lot of walking. Maybe also get a new shirt for Farsheed. Her phone vibrated with the promise of a text.

Happy holidays was all it said. Time to start researching the target whose name she had memorized in Tehran. It was easy to recall because all she had to do was ask if he 'had a fish?' and it was forever engraved on her brain. She walked in what looked like the right direction to the shops, removing the SIM card as she went and dropping it between two parked cars into a drain.

SIXTEEN

When a long-held fear becomes reality after years of being just an unrealized fear, you would expect some release, thought Julian. A cathartic liberation from your worst imaginings. If he had expected freedom from the anxiety that had been festering in the back of his mind – festering ever since he had quit British Aerospace in 1988 and Boris had gone back to what was still the USSR – he was wrong. He had always dreaded seeing Boris again, or being confronted by someone who knew something of his past. Every time he met someone new, or was approached in the street, or asked an innocuous question (like Cassie asking if he's been to Moscow), it was there, like a tumour in his brain. But all that seemed to have happened was that the fear had now spread to his whole being. He was going around as if in a surreal and unpleasant dream that he could not wake from. Sleep was disrupted by night sweats and his gut was worse than ever.

After meeting Boris, once home, he'd barely spoken to Sheila for fear he'd unwittingly tell her what had happened, and was able only to send a late-night text telling Rami his U-turn decision.

Rami was pleased, but seemed incurious as to why, after so much argument, Julian had given in. But that was just as well, because Julian wasn't sure how he could explain it. So the following day Rami came into his office with a happy grin on his face. He closed the door and carefully placed a Jiffy bag on Julian's desk before sitting opposite.

Julian had been shy as a child; girls had terrified him and he hated being called on by the teacher in class. Things had improved as he'd stumbled into adulthood, but he still considered himself an introvert and was happiest working on his own. He let Rami handle the presentations for pitches, although he was always there to explain the technical stuff, but contentment came when getting into the code with the developers, or even better, having a go himself. Which is why, over the next forty-eight hours, when it became apparent what Boris wanted, part of him couldn't help but relish the potential work involved. Besides, he had decided that the best way to get rid of Boris was to do what he asked as quickly as he could.

Within the padded safety of the Jiffy bag was a circuit board, no bigger than the size of a very thin paperback, and two pages of badly written requirements that could be boiled down to: is this system robust? In other words, could someone take over the drone using fake GPS signals and control it themselves? This rang a bell with Julian, and an Internet search revealed an article in which Iran claimed that they had taken over a pilotless CIA drone and landed it in Iran. He watched footage of it, virtually intact, shown on Iranian TV. An Iranian engineer said that they had exploited a weakness in the GPS navigation system – which is the most vulnerable part of the drone – and broadcast their own GPS coordinates to it, fooling it into landing on their territory. Boris had mentioned Iran when they'd met, but he was unclear as to whom he was now working for, if anyone. It sounded like he was trying to line his own pockets, to build a nest egg for his old age, which he seemed to be slipping into rather ungraciously. He was probably making use of his vast network and acting as a paid consultant. The best, if not only, option open to Julian was to get the job done and dusted and let Boris move on and out of his life. He plugged the circuit board into his laptop and fired up some debugging software that allowed him to see what was on it.

He was so engrossed in what he was doing that he was surprised to see Naomi standing before his desk holding a sandwich and a steaming cardboard cup; he hadn't heard her come in despite the door being closed.

'Sorry to bother you. You've been cooped up since this morning and it's past lunch so I thought you might want something.' She put the food and drink on his desk.

Julian looked at his watch; it was two in the afternoon. 'Thanks, I lost track of time.'

She smiled and went to the door, where she hesitated. 'I saw Rami in here this morning and I was just wondering whether you'd asked him about, you know, that thing we talked about. I'm keen to get them off to the accountants.'

'The expenses. Sorry, I've been really busy the last couple of days. Is he there now?'

'No, he left before lunch.'

'OK. I promise I'll do it as soon as I'm done with this piece of work.'

Once she was gone Julian unwrapped his freshly made sandwich. The coffee was black and sugarless, just as he liked it. He'd forgotten about the money thing, justifiably, and made a mental note to speak to Rami when he next saw him. He settled back to his reading.

Julian's initial idea of what Boris wanted was slightly off target. What the UAV designers had done was to compensate for the possibility of GPS spoofing – i.e. taking over the GPS signal and controlling the UAV – by introducing other ways of tracking it in the form of movement detectors (gyroscopes and accelerometers) which were used to determine the physical path of the UAV independently from the GPS system. So if there was a discrepancy between the two systems it could adjust the flight path accordingly, or alert an operator via a data satellite link. It looked like a sensible approach, but the key thing was whether they had got the maths right and what parameters were used when this compensation was done on board, as the dangers of accumulated error could lead to drift.

Flying a drone was like blindfolding someone, setting them off in a straight line towards a door, then nudging them off their path ever so slightly. Every time you did that and the person tried to adjust their direction towards where they thought they should be going, it introduced a new error. So it was with UAVs, and a bit of mathematics was needed to minimize this error by deciding which measurements to use according to their certainty. By averaging out the errors, it could work out any corrections needed to the trajectory. As this process was recursive – measurements taken, corrections made, new measurements taken, etc. – this could all be done in real time.

So far so good, Julian thought. He had a good understanding of the overall system. He reached for his coffee. It was cold. His sandwich was half-eaten. He looked at the clock on the wall: 18.45. Through his door he could see the main office was empty except for a cleaner hoovering the carpet. He unplugged the circuit board from his laptop and put it back in its bag. Rami had said it wasn't to leave the office, but Julian felt happier if he had it with him. Besides, he would probably want to check something later on, probably in the middle of the night when it woke him up. As he locked up and turned off the lights he felt a slight pang of disappointment that Naomi hadn't said goodnight before she'd left.

SEVENTEEN

Mojgan lay face down on the bed in just a T-shirt, trying to forget her failed evening by sliding her right hand between her legs, thighs pressed hard together. She was thinking of Farsheed but there were voices in the hotel corridor, people passing her door. She gave up and got under the covers. She wanted desperately to ring him, to hear his voice. She pictured him in the kitchen of their small Tehran apartment, located in the Zafaraniyeh area of the city near a synagogue and just a thirty-minute walk from one of the residential houses owned by the Ministry of Intelligence. It was there that she, Farsheed and others all worked surrounded by servers, network cable and terminals.

Apart from the bedroom, it was the kitchen where Farsheed

liked to spend his time, making *adas polow* or other dishes picked up from his father. How Farsheed had wangled the apartment – in one of the most affluent areas of Tehran – was unclear to Mojgan, but she saw it as one of the perks of his technical expertise and rapid rise in the organization. Many of their neighbours were, like them, abroad a lot of the time, and Farsheed and Mojgan informed them that they did business in Europe, and that they were in 'computers'. This was true to an extent, and since many of their neighbours were also in business, they didn't question it. The area was a far cry from the less well-to-do east of the city where the Ministry of Intelligence building was situated, somewhere Farsheed often had to go and report.

In the hot Tehran summer, since they were not overlooked, Farsheed would often walk around the place naked. Especially after making love. He would laugh at her for calling it that, but she could not call it what he called it, although she liked to hear his crude utterances when they were in physical union. Her hand moved down over her belly. She closed her eyes, thinking of his voice. But again, there were people in the hall, women this time, coming back from a night out, loud with alcohol, their laughter uncouth.

She got out of bed and went to the window. She had moved to a hotel on a corner of Euston Square, opposite Euston Station, and was on the top floor. She could see Euston Square down below. London seemed to be full of small patches of green like this. A steady stream of cars drove on the Euston Road despite it being after midnight. The hotel was perfectly placed; it took fifteen minutes to walk round the back streets, underneath the railway tracks leading into St Pancras – where she had arrived on the train – and emerge on to York Way, home of Hadfish Systems. She had established yesterday, via the Hadfish website, that there were two directors of Hadfish Systems. One, an Englishman with a sad face, was the technical director; the other, a Lebanese Christian, judging by his name, was head of business development. There was only one other named employee, an office manager, and apart from her the rest of the company was identified only by a photo of an open-plan office with a dozen programmers, two of them women, staring at screens. The Englishman was definitely the most likely target, or maybe one of the more experienced coders. There were no vacancies at the firm, which would have been the easiest way of getting inside the place.

So that morning she had reconnoitred the offices. The ground floor and entrance to the five-storey building consisted of a shared reception area complete with a bored-looking receptionist. From her Mojgan had established, by pretending to look for a cleaning job, that the whole building was cleaned at night by a company contracted by the building owners. Since most cleaners in Europe were dark-skinned in her experience, this had been her next plan of action: go in as one and be invisible – another brown person in a uniform ignored by everyone. If she'd had time she could have tried applying for a job with the cleaning company but there was no guarantee she would be sent to the building or, even if she was, that she would be asked to clean Hadfish rather than one of the other offices occupying the building. Sometimes, she thought, hacking into somewhere was easier than physically getting in. Realizing that she was standing at the window only in her T-shirt, she pulled the curtains across and got back into bed.

She needed to rethink her next move after her earlier failure that evening. At around seven thirty she'd taken up a position down the road from Hadfish towards King's Cross station and waited. Gradually, in dribs and drabs, the cleaners came up York Way, walking rather than taking the short bus ride, probably to save money. They were distinguishable by the grey and blue tunics they wore over their clothes. She'd waited, looking for the right person, not sure who the right person was, except someone who looked vaguely similar, someone whose ID photo wouldn't look too different. One of the things she'd noticed earlier in the day was that unless you had an appointment and signed in at the reception, you needed a swipe card to get through to the lifts. She'd felt nervous; she was happier sitting at a computer and probing weaknesses that way. But, as Farsheed was fond of saying, change involved action in the real world, not just the virtual.

Then she saw the young woman in the headscarf. Mojgan took out her own scarf and put it on. With her hair covered they looked similar enough.

As she approached, Mojgan smiled, saying, 'Salaam, sister.' The woman had slowed up but did not stop.

'*Wa 'alaiki al-salaam*,' she'd said, smiling but alert, steetwise.

'Are you going to work at the offices there?' Mojgan had asked, pointing to the glass building up the road and walking alongside.

The woman had nodded warily.

'I was wondering, sister, whether I could borrow your ID card and uniform in return for a hundred pounds?'

'A hundred pounds?' The woman had then said something in Arabic that Mojgan hadn't understood.

'I will return the card,' Mojgan had said. 'I just want to get into the offices and leave a message for my . . . sweetheart, you know? I will be twenty minutes.'

'Where are you from?' the woman had asked.

Mojgan had hesitated. 'Turkey. The love of my life works in the building but I am forbidden to see him by my parents. I just want to leave a letter on his desk,' she'd said slowly.

The woman had thought about it, studying her, then nodded. 'I know. Why don't you tell me which office he works in and I will leave the letter on his desk.'

The woman had spoken quickly in a strange English accent, and it had taken Mojgan a moment to be wrong-footed by what she'd heard; she hadn't considered the possibility of a cleaner turning down money with a sensible and helpful response.

'Where does he work? Which company?' the woman had asked.

'Hadfish Systems,' Mojgan had said, buying time to think.

'Yes, I know it. On the top floor?'

Mojgan had nodded – that much she knew from the signs in reception.

'Is he in the open-plan bit or in one of the side offices?'

Mojgan had remembered the photo of the office and calculated that the directors would have their own offices, so she'd chosen the latter. 'But it is better if I go myself because I don't know which office. Maybe you could give me your card. I'll be ten minutes.'

'No,' the woman had said, shaking her head. 'Anyway, the

side offices are locked. We don't have access unless there is someone from the company there. Maybe I could put it under the door for you?' She had started to walk more quickly and Mojgan had realized she was losing the woman's belief in her story. She'd briefly considered making some appeal to her as a Muslim, explaining what she was trying to do and how it might help Muslims everywhere, or perhaps trying one of the other cleaners, but she had already drawn too much attention to herself. Instead, she'd let her walk off. Approaching someone else no longer being an option, she'd walked the streets back to her hotel in low spirits.

She had to find a way in to Hadfish, and at least she'd learnt that it had to be when the directors were there during the day. She put the bedside light on and switched on the small netbook she'd bought from the computer shop on Tottenham Court Road, connected to the Internet and brought up the Hadfish website using a dongle and a proxy connection that cloaked her IP address. Perhaps there was something on the site that she had missed that might suggest a new approach.

The arrow on the screen that mimicked her forefinger movements on the trackpad alighted on the office manager's photo. An older black woman. An office manager, Mojgan thought, was simply a glorified way of describing a secretary, a position that seemed to be viewed with some disdain in the West. Typing documents in English was something Mojgan was more than capable of doing. A couple of years of transcribing the recorded conversations of visiting foreigners might at last pay off.

EIGHTEEN

A week after meeting Cassie, Sheila was waiting for her at an outside café on the King's Road near the Saatchi Gallery. She felt contented, people-watching from behind sunglasses with the late-morning sun on her shoulders. She reflected on a tough week. Jules had become yet more withdrawn, staying late at the office (although she couldn't get hold of him one evening) and saying only that he'd agreed, after all, to take on the Rami job that they'd been squabbling about. She'd catch him staring at her as if deciding something. She wanted to prompt him, get him to open up, but she was half-afraid of what he might say, her old fears of him confiding in someone else resurfacing.

She brought herself back to the here-and-now as a woman wearing oversized sunglasses and a fitted red dress approached, carrying a large designer-labelled shopping bag. She looked much like many of the women who shopped on the King's Road and it took Sheila a second to recognize Cassie. She'd changed her hair; it looked longer, with contrasting highlights. Cassie put the bag down next to the table and whipped off her glasses.

'Sheila!' she exclaimed, as if they were old friends. Sheila took off her sunglasses too and stood up. Cassie embraced her, then unashamedly checked her out. 'Lovely trousers,' she said, pulling out a chair. 'Linen?'

Sheila nodded, gesturing at the matching jacket on the back of her chair. She wasn't sure why she'd agreed to meet with Cassie, who'd rung her out of the blue. 'I got your number from Rami,' she'd told Sheila on the phone, 'I hope you don't mind.' How could she mind? Cassie's cheerfulness had come at just the right time, and the fact that she was nothing like her friends was probably a factor in agreeing to meet. She needed something less demanding than yet another analysis of the latest film or book and the endless talk about children, which most of her circle were now encumbered by. At times she felt her whole social scene to be terribly narrow and suffocating. Also, truth be told, she was curious about Cassie, and what Rami saw in her beyond the obvious.

'What have you been buying?' Sheila asked, as Cassie flashed a smile at the waiter.

'Shoes,' she said. She ordered an iced coffee and leant forward to rummage in the bag. She took out a pair of high heels and put them on the table between them.

Strappy 'fuck-me' shoes was all Sheila could think. 'Very nice,' was what she said.

'Three hundred and twenty-nine pounds of foot-deforming shoe,' Cassie said, putting them away.

'How was Moscow?' Sheila asked, wondering whether this get-together was such a good idea after all.

'A hoot, as always,' Cassie said, ignoring the waiter as he set her drink down. 'How's Julian? Rami says he's working on this new contract. You know, the one they were arguing about.'

'Yes, although I don't know what it is. Apparently it's confidential.'

'Rami says it's for an arms company, but that's all. Something to do with, what do you call them, UAVs. I can't remember what that stands for. Unmanned something. Anyway, they call them drones. It's something to do with drones and GPS, you know, like the thing you have in your car.'

'That's Julian's thing, GPS. But an arms company?' So that's what Rami meant at dinner about Jules having principles, she thought. Also, it was a little galling that Rami told Cassie what the job is but Jules didn't tell her. Yet another example of him withholding.

'I take it he doesn't want to work for an arms company?' Cassie asked, running her fingers through her hair and flicking it off her bare shoulders. Something about Cassie appeared carefully managed, Sheila thought, but not overdone. Something she couldn't quite put her finger on, something that didn't ring true, other than the silicone enhancements. Perhaps it was all part of being in PR, creating an image.

'He worked for British Aerospace for years and hated it. The macho culture, the weapons they made, the way they got round arms embargoes. He was relieved to leave.'

'So why take this job?'

'I don't know. I can't talk to him at the moment. It's stressing him out but there's not a lot I can do about it. He refuses to talk about it.'

Cassie leant forward and raised her lovely eyebrows, which to Sheila looked unpruned, unlike a lot of eyebrows you saw around here. 'Everything all right in the bedroom department, is it?'

Sheila felt herself blush. 'That's usually not a problem, but when he's stressed like this he loses interest. I think that's pretty normal, though.'

Cassie turned down her mouth as if doubtful. 'If he's losing interest in you then he's got problems. You don't think he's seeing someone else, do you?'

Sheila was so taken aback at the casual manner in which the question was asked that it was a moment before she realized she was sitting with her mouth open. 'That's a bit of a leap from—'

Cassie's mobile, sitting by her plate, emitted a joyful tune – an instrumental version of a current pop song. She picked it up and examined the screen. 'Sorry, I have to take this, it's work.'

Sheila picked up her own phone to check for emails and pretend she wasn't listening to Cassie's call, but Cassie didn't seem to care if she was overheard. In fact, she was looking at Sheila all the while she was talking.

'Sure, that's not a problem . . . When? No, that's fine, honestly.' She laughed. 'Yes, that's true . . . OK, bye.' She put her phone away. 'Sorry about that, what were we talking about?'

'Do you like your job?' Sheila asked, keen to change the subject.

'Sometimes, depends on the clients. It takes me places I wouldn't otherwise go. It pays really, really well, which means if I'm careful I can quit in a few years.'

'Three hundred and fifty pounds' worth of shoes isn't being careful,' Sheila said.

'True, true. But you have to look the part in my business.'

Sheila wanted to ask whether she thought people didn't take her seriously, dressing like that, but she lacked Cassie's forward nature.

'So you're telling me it's never crossed your mind, whether Julian is seeing someone else?'

'Not really,' Sheila lied. It had occurred to her plenty of times.

'The thing is it's easy enough to find out.'

'What?'

Cassie placed a soft hand on Sheila's. Her fingernails were immaculately French-manicured. 'He wouldn't be the first, would he? If they're unhappy in one aspect of their lives they think the solution is found in another,' she said, pointing to her lap with her free hand. It took Sheila a second to understand what she meant. Cassie patted the back of Sheila's hand for emphasis. 'Believe me, I know.'

Sheila shook her head. 'I think he's just absorbed with the

job, that's all. Struggling with it because he didn't really want to do it.' She slipped her hand from under Cassie's and hid her uneven nails in her lap.

'Rami tells me that you guys have been together for years, that you even got engaged at one point.'

Just how much else had Rami bloody told her? Sheila wondered. But looking at Cassie's light blue eyes she just saw ingenuous curiosity. 'Yes, we did get engaged a couple of years after university. But we never got disengaged as such.'

'Just didn't follow through?'

Sheila laughed. 'Exactly. We didn't follow through.'

'And no ring?'

'I took it off a while ago, it felt a bit . . .'

Cassie sat up straight and the male waiter appeared magically by their table. Cassie's enhancements, emphasized by the perfect fit of her dress, provided benefits that Sheila hadn't appreciated. 'Let's go to lunch,' Cassie said enthusiastically, and without waiting for an answer threw too much cash on the table and stood up.

A thirty-pound bottle of chilled Chablis and a Caesar salad later and Cassie was telling Sheila that Rami was too serious about their relationship for her liking.

'The proverbial clock is ticking. I want to have a kid, sooner rather than later.'

'But not with Rami?'

She snorted. 'I know he's a friend of yours but would you have a child with him?'

Sheila slowly shook her head.

'That's why I work all hours now, so I've got enough to quit work down the road. I'll have enough put by to do it on my own, so who knows, I might visit a sperm bank.'

'I knew you would.'

'What, visit a sperm bank?'

'No, I mean I knew you valued your financial independence.'

'Of course.' She drained her glass. 'Men are too needy.'

'More than women, you think?'

'Oh, yes, or in a different way. They need . . . reassuring all the time. I suppose they're a bit like children in that respect. Shall I order more wine?'

'God, no, I've got work to do this afternoon,' Sheila said, thinking that actually she could do with some reassurance herself.

'Houses to sell?'

'No, I volunteer at the hospital once a week, so I need coffee and chewing gum.' She waved at a waiter.

'I'm impressed. I could never do anything like that.'

'Well, I didn't think I could either until a few months ago.'

'What made you do it?'

'I'm not sure. I just felt my life was too . . . I don't know, restricted, small, not fully lived, if that makes sense?' she asked, embarrassed despite the inhibition-loosening effects of the wine.

Cassie made a sympathetic face but obviously had no clue what Sheila was talking about. 'So kids weren't an option for you two?'

Sheila was getting used to Cassie's bluntness, and grateful that she wasn't pretending kids could still be a real possibility at her age.

'At some point they were, maybe. Maybe they would have filled a gap, maybe they would have completed things, but maybe that would've been the wrong reason to have any. There's something more . . . I can't really explain it, to be honest. Anyway,' she added, aware she was repeating herself, 'if a kid is really what you want, Cassie, then don't leave it too late.'

Cassie took Sheila's hands and leant forward. 'The clock is ticking. You could come with me to the sperm bank and help me choose.' They laughed and ordered coffee from the waiter while still holding hands, and the not unpleasant thought came to Sheila that the waiter, a woman, might think them a couple, with Cassie being Sheila's younger trophy girlfriend. She felt giddy with the wine and the intimacy; she'd never discussed not having kids with her friends before, simply because no one had asked her, and yet here she was opening up to someone she hardly knew and had very little in common with.

She recovered her now clammy hands. 'I wanted to ask you . . .' she started saying.

'You can ask me anything, darling,' Cassie said, encouragingly.

'You said earlier, that it would be easy to find out, you know, whether . . .'

'Whether he's seeing someone else?'

Sheila hardly nodded and Cassie said, businesslike, 'It'll take a weight off your mind and he'll never know.'

'I'm not sure I could do it. You know, the actual practicalities. It's like a betrayal in itself.'

Cassie smiled and patted Sheila's hand. 'Just leave it to me, Sheila. We girls have to stick together.'

NINETEEN

Julian, rubbing his eyes and stroking his stubble, had become intrigued by some comments in the code on the circuit board. Mainly because he couldn't read them. They were just empty squares or random symbols. The comments in a program were there to explain a section or line of code, both as a reminder to the programmer of what that piece of code did or, more importantly, an explanation to the next programmer taken on to make changes or updates. It was good practice to include these comments, and they were enclosed in special characters that made them invisible to the computer running the code but obvious to a human. Except the ones in the control unit routines were unreadable to Julian. He wondered if they were deliberately ciphered, given this was a military job, but he didn't have time to worry about it, and in a sense it forced him to work through it blind rather than being falsely reassured by bad documentation. Instead he chunked the code down, concentrating on working through each routine by taking it through the debugging software then making a note when a different part of the program was called so he could check that later. It was tedious and complex work, since the routines were dependent on many variables being fed in by sensors on the aircraft. So he put on some Bach, which always seemed to enhance his concentration. Many coders listened to music as they worked, some of it dreadful heavy metal or techno stuff.

Each to his own, and if he walked through the open-plan office at Hadfish he was treated to a cacophony of tinny sounds coming from the headphones (again in a variety of styles) of the coders, who could spend hours hunched over a screen without coming up for air. Julian, however, was at an age where he needed a regular break, and he pulled off his headphones to stretch his legs and use the toilet.

It was late again and most of the coders were gone. Nizar was there, shutting down his workstation and retying his long hair at the back. He hooked his laptop rucksack over one shoulder and turned to see Julian. He came over to the office as Julian opened his door.

'How's it going, boss?' he asked. 'You look busy.'

'I like to keep my hand in. Can't let you young guys have all the fun.'

'What you working on?'

'It's a control board for a GPS tracking system,' Julian said, keeping things general. 'Why are you here so late?'

'There's a lot to pick up.'

'Enjoying it?'

'Of course. I love getting stuck in to new challenges. It's all problem-solving, isn't it, at the end of the day?'

'Exactly, always using the most efficient lines of code, of course.'

They smiled and Julian realized he was missing basic human company. He wanted to get home to Sheila but, as Nizar turned to go, he remembered something. 'I've got a little problem for you to solve,' he said, 'if you're not in a hurry?'

Nizar removed his rucksack and put it down. 'Lead me to it, boss.'

Julian reckoned there was little Nizar could glean from seeing a few lines of code, so he led him to his desk and swivelled his screen around. He pointed to some of the missing or garbled comments. 'What do you think is going on there?'

Nizar peered at the screen. 'Is this like a test?'

'No, I'm genuinely asking for your help.'

He nodded and said, 'OK. So that's Linux. The rubbish looks like it should be the comments, right?' He was tentative. 'Not code. I mean, each line starts with a hash symbol.'

'Yep.'

'This is too easy, unless it's a trick question?'

'No.'

'Well, I've come across this before, these squares. It's because it's written in a language you haven't got installed on your laptop. I've worked on some programs written by Arab programmers and they sometimes put in a few comments in Arabic, you know, like a signature thing. I had to download the Arabic language file so I could read them.'

Julian slapped his forehead and laughed at his own stupidity.

'Was I wrong?' Nizar asked.

'No, no, I've just been sitting in front of the screen too long,' Julian said.

Nizar looked pleased with himself. 'Shall we see what language it's in?' he asked, reaching for the keyboard.

Julian grabbed his arm. Nizar was thin and wiry. 'No, you get off. I'll sort it out. Well done, Nizar. It had been nagging me.'

'Pleased to be of help, boss,' he said, grinning and picking up his rucksack.

'By the way, I keep meaning to ask you,' Julian said as he went back to his chair. 'I've noticed you and your mates, down at the café, hunched over your laptops every lunchtime. It's none of my business what you get up to in your spare time, but I'm curious; you guys working on something?'

Nizar stood at the door, taking a moment to answer. 'Well, just something to make the world a better place,' he said, straight-faced.

Julian, bemused and intrigued, wanted to ask him more, but he'd already left in a bit of a hurry, as if regretting saying anything at all. He figured they were working on a game that they hoped would go viral and make them rich. He'd been there in his youth.

Back at his laptop, Julian established that the operating system had been stripped of all languages except English, possibly in a bid to save space. He quit the debugger, downloaded a multi-language pack from the web and installed it. Then he restarted the machine and fired up the debugger. The gaps were magically filled.

'Nizar, you're a fucking genius.'

He couldn't understand a word that it said, but he knew Hebrew when he saw it. Now he understood why Boris was banging on about being Jewish: he was working for Israel.

TWENTY

S heila hadn't had a chance to tell Julian about her meeting with Gulnar because he just hadn't been around, but she had followed it up with some productive action. Thus her impetuous decision to help set up this charity for amputee children had taken a further step towards reality. After several weeks of being a patient support volunteer, which involved visiting patients and acting as an advocate, she'd met a very young Afghani girl brought to the UK for surgery after her legs had been blown off below the knee by a cluster bomb. Her trip had been arranged by an enthusiastic young occupational therapist, Gulnar, who'd been working in Afghanistan. She'd shared with Sheila her vision of being able to fly therapists, equipped with prosthetics and know-how, over to war zones to 'literally get people back on their feet'. Gulnar, who was of Afghani heritage on her mother's side, was self-aware enough to know that she didn't have the organizational know-how to pull it off. Sheila immediately recognized how her own skills might be useful. She may not have the idealism, or even the ideas, but she saw no shame in latching on to someone else's, someone who was more altruistically minded than she, someone who knew how to engage with the world in a way she was struggling to discover. She could, of course, just have given Gulnar some money to help out, but that would have provided little satisfaction; she'd given enough of the stuff away every time some appeal came up on the TV, or when she was stopped in the street by a charity worker. But she realized that what she really wanted was to have that personal contact that Gulnar was talking about, even if it meant stepping out of her comfort zone, which is why she'd become a volunteer in the first place.

She put the early evening TV news on. There was a report

from Pakistan about a drone strike which caught her interest because it was on the border with Afghanistan. The report was patchy in detail, some mobile phone footage showing a large crater where some houses had been, locals saying no al-Qaeda were present, just civilians. She switched off the TV and went upstairs to the computer to research UAVs, or drones as they were colloquially known.

Glued to the Internet, studying a subject sparked by a conversation with Cassie, no less, she tried (unsuccessfully) to avoid thinking about whether she'd actually agreed that Cassie would arrange to have Julian spied upon, to check if he was seeing another woman. It must have been the wine, the moment, Cassie making the suggestion so matter-of-factly. Now she regretted agreeing to it. It was underhand, which made her uncomfortable. It wasn't just holding stuff back from him like the volunteering; it was being proactively underhand.

Since it was approaching five thirty she went down to the kitchen, poured herself some white wine from the fridge and headed back upstairs to the small bedroom she had turned into an office, which many years ago she'd secretly planned as a nursery. Maybe she could call the detective thing off. She looked at her phone, newly programmed with Cassie's mobile number. Maybe Cassie had forgotten about it. If so, to phone her would make it real and embarrass them both. At least this way she had some deniability. Fuck, what was she thinking? She tried to put it from her mind by going back to the screen and concentrating on something of importance. She'd allowed her life to be thrown off-kilter by a younger woman with fake boobs. Maybe, she thought, clicking on yet another video of the after-effects of a drone strike, Third World problems could drown out First World ones.

An hour of watching videos and reading articles made Sheila's brain hurt. The beginning of a headache was creeping up from the back of her neck. She'd suspected for a while that she needed reading glasses but had repeatedly put off going to the opticians. Her solution to the headache was a couple of painkillers washed down with more wine. She took her refreshed glass and a sheaf of printouts out on to the patio where the sun was low in the cloud-free western sky. Her research into drones had borne unpleasant fruit. They were used everywhere, well, in lands mostly far away, and had become the weapon of choice in the war on terror, operating in countries where no war had been declared, on suspects (usually dark-skinned) who had not been convicted of anything by any court. Even if one could stomach that, the rate of what was euphemistically called collateral damage, meaning the civilians killed or injured in these attacks, was high, and that was when they hit the right targets. She had numerous press reports in front of her of innocent groups of people, often children, being blown to pieces, often hit by a second missile when going to help the victims of the first – so-called 'double-tap' strikes. The reports of killed civilians followed a depressing pattern. Initially dismissed by the US government, they would be subsequently modified when facts on the ground became available. It was as if they deliberately started from a position of denial until they saw what reports from the area emerged.

She could see the appeal of this unmanned combat to politicians, since it didn't involve sending voters or their loved ones to face death, and there was zero accountability. She couldn't really understand why Julian was getting involved in working on such a thing, especially since he seemed to have objected to it earlier, if that snippet she'd heard at dinner with Rami was anything to go by. It's not that he was overtly political, or banged on about his principles, if he had any. They never really talked politics, but, like most other people, they shared a cynicism about anything to do with the political system. One thing that she had admired him for was his stepping aside from a promising career at British Aerospace Systems to set up with Rami. Perhaps Rami had just worn him down about it in the end; he could be very persuasive.

She checked her watch and went to prepare some dinner, even though she didn't have much hope that Julian would be back in time. As she chopped an onion to make a tomato sauce, she wondered whether she shouldn't have taken more interest in his work, tried at least to understand it. But the computer games stuff had turned her off. War games, they always seemed to be. Always about killing. She'd once been at a friend's house and remembered being quietly horrified when watching her friend's son and some friends play at killing on the TV screen. 'Boys have always played at war,' his father had said when she'd commented on it, 'now it's just computerized.' And more real, Sheila had thought, more graphic. In fact, the game had very much resembled the remote-controlled missile attacks they'd shown footage of when invading Iraq. It was all done once-removed, on a screen. She remembered that Wikileaks video that was released online, of the pilots targeting some civilians they believed to be acting suspiciously. Their comments had been those of teenagers playing a video game. They probably hadn't been much more than teenagers themselves, could even have grown up playing the same video game she'd watched those boys play.

She stirred her tomato sauce while calling Hadfish with her mobile but it just rang. She tried Julian's mobile, not expecting an answer.

'Hi.' He sounded breathy, like he was walking and talking.

'Oh, hi. Are you on your way home?'

'Yes, just heading to the car.'

'Oh, good. I've got dinner on.'

'Great. I'll see you in twenty or thirty minutes.'

It was amazing how one could be cheered by a simple, inconsequential call, Sheila thought, as she set the small table in the kitchen. She found and lit the red candles she used to create what Julian, a little mockingly, called 'an ambience'. She'd printed out some stuff from her research ready to have a discussion about drones. Maybe she wouldn't ask him about it tonight. Maybe they could have some wine and make love and she could reclaim him that way, just for a while, just to prove to herself that she could. She felt a pang of remorse when remembering her conversation with Cassie. What if he found out about it? But how could he? While the water boiled for the pasta she went upstairs and checked her face. She thought about changing into something he might find more alluring but it seemed a little contrived. The whole idea of having to make herself alluring made her feel tired. She was overthinking, again. It's what he said she did. He was right – even though it was a little of the pot calling the kettle black – but she found it difficult not to, especially after some wine.

Back in the kitchen she checked the time and put on the pasta; he'd be here any minute. Eleven minutes later he had still not arrived. Another twenty minutes elapsed and she gave up trying to keep the pasta warm. Thirty minutes later she blew the candles out and put them away. The white-wine bottle was empty and she considered opening the red she'd got out. But she was too comfortable to get up and go into the kitchen. Forty-five minutes after putting the pasta on she heard his key in the door and he came into the living room. He looked pale.

'Sorry I'm late.'

'What happened?'

'I got waylaid by one of the developers. Caught me as I was leaving.'

'I thought you were in the car park when I rang?' She was enunciating her words carefully so she didn't sound like she'd been drinking, but he seemed too preoccupied to notice.

He took off his jacket, revealing sweat stains at his armpits. 'No, I was just leaving the office. We've got this new guy, remember, I mentioned him? Nizar. He needs handholding.' He put his jacket over the back of the sofa, looked at the empty bottle of wine but not at her, and went into the kitchen. She was pleased she hadn't changed after all; she would have looked pathetic.

'You didn't wait, I hope?' he shouted above his clattering.

'No, I bloody didn't,' she said.

'Sorry, I didn't catch that.'

She pulled herself out of the sofa and made her way upstairs to bed. She was too tired to confront him about drones.

TWENTY-ONE

Mojgan's training, before moving to the cyber-monitoring unit Farsheed had set up, had included some actual eyes-on-the-target surveillance, but it was not her specialty, and doing it on your own was problematic and increased the risk of being spotted. Three or four people, at least, were needed to avoid the possibility of detection. But since

Naomi was a civilian, and unlikely to suspect that she was even being followed, Mojgan assumed there would be little risk of being spotted if she were careful. Mojgan was more concerned that she'd have to negotiate the London Tube system when she picked up Naomi leaving Hadfish and tailed her down York Way towards King's Cross. But Naomi had crossed the Euston Road and gone down a side street, then through a small park with a tennis court where she'd lingered, seemingly to admire some aspect of nature. She sat at a bench and Mojgan had to wonder whether this was a sign of counter-surveillance. Mojgan walked slowly round the perimeter, keeping Naomi's back in view. After a few minutes she got up and left the way Mojgan had. Mojgan followed her on to a narrow street lined with four-storey red-brick buildings that looked newly built. Naomi disappeared into one of them, and when Mojgan reached it she discovered a barred gate, locked, with a bank of eight doorbells embedded in the wall to its left. Doorbells with no names beside them.

Last night she had ached physically for Farsheed; now she yearned for him professionally. She had come here with no real plan except some vague idea about overpowering the woman, who was a lot older, then perhaps stealing her security card and office keys, buying just enough time to get into Hadfish and do what she needed to do. It was weak, Mojgan knew that; what if she had a husband, or children, for instance? Never mind her abhorrence of physical violence; she just wasn't physically or mentally built for it. But she'd been informed, via her online word game, that she needed to get on with it. Farsheed had asked her – although she knew he was being pressured by his own superiors – whether they needed to send help, by which she understood someone who could undertake the things she was reluctant to. That, she knew, would be damaging to Farsheed, an admission of failure, never mind the involvement of other departments.

Someone had appeared on the other side of the gate – an old woman holding a tiny dog with bulging eyes. She smiled at Mojgan as the gate squeaked open, a quizzical tilt to her head. Mojgan made sure she smiled back, her finger hovering over the glowing buzzers.

'I have forgotten what apartment Naomi is in,' she said.

'Flat four,' the old woman said, holding the gate open. Mojgan went in and climbed the stairs, discovering that there were two apartments per floor, much like her building back home. Reaching the second she hesitated by number four. How to approach this? Perhaps she would try something she was comfortable with first. She took her netbook from her bag, aware of the handgun in the bottom, wrapped in her headscarf. Opening the computer, she scanned for wireless networks. There were three, the one with the strongest signal, which still had what looked like the generic name that came with the modem, being unprotected. She sat on the floor outside the door and fired up some software that could capture the wireless traffic between it and the lone computer connected to it. It was encrypted, but forcing a disconnect with her software meant she could capture the moment the computer (conveniently called 'Naomi's computer') reconnected with the router. There it all was, not even a password to login. Incredible. Now she could start to peel Naomi's onion. How impressed you'd be, Farsheed, if you could see me now.

TWENTY-TWO

When Julian got to Hadfish he put his briefcase on his desk and went straight next door into Rami's office, intending to talk to him about the unexplained cash withdrawals. A petite dark-skinned woman, rather beautiful in his eyes, was standing before Rami's desk. Rami leant back in his chair, hands locked behind his head, elbows akimbo. He had that slight smile Julian had seen him reserve for women, an affected grin that he probably thought looked charming, and most probably women found it so. Julian envied Rami his ease with the opposite sex; he could somehow be tactile and flirtatious without causing offence, even making Sheila giggle – something Julian couldn't seem to manage. Julian found that despite himself he was grinning stupidly at this woman, such was her appeal.

'This is Salma,' Rami said with pride, as if he had invented her. Salma put some post on Rami's desk and stuck her childlike hand out. Julian was conscious not to squeeze it too hard.

'You must be Julian Fisher,' she said. 'I'll go and get your mail.' She moved past him to the doorway.

'Who's that?' he asked Rami once she had gone and he'd closed the door behind her.

'Naomi's replacement,' Rami said, looking past Julian into the open office.

'Where's Naomi? She hasn't got holiday booked, has she?'

'No, she's off sick, but she arranged a replacement from the agency.'

'Sick? Naomi's never off sick. What's wrong with her?' Rami shrugged and Julian contained his exasperation; sometimes Rami exhibited no natural curiosity.

'OK, never mind, although why does everyone say mail now, instead of post?'

'You're beginning to sound your age,' Rami said, picking up the stack of envelopes Salma had put on his desk.

Julian plonked himself in the chair next to the door. 'I need to talk to you about something.'

'I'm listening.' He slit open an envelope and started to read, glancing up at Julian expectantly, giving him half of his attention.

'I've been looking at some expense statements for last month, and I've got some questions.'

Rami put down his post and switched over to his desktop.

'It's regarding the expenses credit card.'

Rami's face, which Julian was watching, changed just for a second as he looked at the screen, but it could have been a reaction to something in his inbox. He turned an open expression on Julian. 'And?'

'There have been some cash withdrawals on your card, which is pretty unusual. Nearly three-and-a-half K if memory serves. And a couple of withdrawals in Leeds, if that rings any bells?'

He scrunched up his face. 'No, it doesn't. I probably made a couple of cash withdrawals on the account, but nothing of that amount. What of it?'

'Well, apart from the fact they charge us for withdrawing cash, there are no receipts corresponding to the amounts.'

'I'll make sure I use the card properly next time. Anything else?'

Julian wasn't sure how far to push it; after all, he had other things to worry about. 'Was it for entertaining the UAV job clients? Didn't you say they were based in Leeds?'

'No. Maybe, I can't remember.' A pause. 'I might have taken some cash out in Leeds.'

'Have you learnt anything more about them?'

'Not really. They do a lot of military work.'

'Did you know the original job came from Israel?'

'Where did you get that from?'

Julian had done a quick Google translate of some of the Hebrew text in the program and ascertained that they were just programming comments. 'So it's true?'

Rami raised his hands and shrugged dismissively. 'I don't know, Julian.'

'If it were from Israel, why would a country with a pretty advanced tech base and sense of paranoia outsource sensitive work abroad?'

Rami blew his cheeks out. 'I don't know. Lots of governments outsource sensitive work to the private sector, especially IT stuff. Maybe the company who outsourced to us have connections there. Does it matter?'

'I don't know, Rami. We don't know if it matters, that's the problem. I don't like working blind.'

Rami ignored Julian's outburst. 'How's the job coming along, anyway?'

'Doesn't it bother you that Lebanon is technically at war with Israel? I mean, they could use a drone on your countrymen.'

Rami sighed. 'Business is business, Julian. You know that's always been my motto. And besides, you know my thoughts on some of my so-called countrymen. So how's it coming?'

Julian swallowed his anger; after all, it wasn't as if he had much choice about the job, he was just getting himself worked up for no purpose whatsoever. 'It's coming. I think I can suggest a few improvements. Nothing fundamental, though.'

'That's great. Remember, this is all about the future of the company' – pointing into the open-plan area – 'and the people out there. We're bound to get a lot of repeat business if we do a good job.'

Julian stood up. 'I'd better get to it, then.' He wanted to ask Rami why he thought he had changed his mind and taken on the job in the end, but he couldn't face another argument with the guy. Probably just another example of his innate disinterest.

Back in his office he switched on his laptop and checked his emails. Nothing from Naomi, and nothing from the temp agency she used when she was away. He looked out at Salma sitting at Naomi's desk and caught her staring at him before she quickly switched her attention to the screen in front of her. Maybe he was out of sorts, maybe it was something about the way she'd looked away, but he dug out the telephone number of the temp agency number and picked up the phone. He got through to someone who told him that the person who dealt with Hadfish was in a meeting and that she would get back to him as soon as she was free. He hooked up the circuit board to the laptop and got to work.

TWENTY-THREE

The back of the taxi was getting untidy, strewn with empty soft-drink cans (alcohol was a rare treat; the outcome of the worrying result of a liver biopsy), a plastic bag full of empty potato crisp bags and sandwich wrappers, a half-eaten box of chocolates (he didn't like the dark ones) and a large bottle of water from which he now took a sip. There were also some dog-eared books with newspaper-strip bookmarks for which a cardboard box served as a makeshift library. Boris's journal was open on his knee and he studied the page. At the top was written *Three Walls*, with the page sub-divided into three sections: a) *Shoah*, b) *Israel* and c) *Election*.

He studied these for a while, looking up whenever someone walked past the tinted windows. He was outside Hadfish again and waiting for everyone to leave the office so he could talk to Julian, who, he knew, would be the last to leave. His Lebanese partner, Rami, had already gone, probably to one of the casinos in town again, most likely the Empire in Leicester Square: it was his favourite place for poker and they had a Tuesday game that started at four p.m. with just a fifty-pound buy-in. He looked down at his journal. Keeping it was a security no-no, but Boris was reaching an age and state of mind where he no longer cared. In fact, he thought that the journal – which never left his side and was locked away if it did – was safer than keeping things on a computer, which only the most paranoid of technical wizardry could make secure. The journal was something he'd started soon after he'd moved to Israel, and it was stuffed full of clippings from newspapers or things he'd printed off, as well as his own musings. He kept a heavy elastic band twice-wound round it to keep everything safe from the prying eyes of the opportunistically curious, and some well-placed strips of paper would fall out of particular pages if it was opened by anyone who didn't do it in a particular way. If his masters were to see what he was collecting he'd be relegated to escorting foreign officials who came to Israel to buy weapons, and the thought of being permanently stuck there gave him the fear of being in a virtual prison.

He looked at the word *Election*, wrote underneath it *Jewish souls*, then decided it would have to wait until he'd done some more reading on the matter, then under *Shoah* wrote: *One long Shoah. 'Never again'. Sacred. Dwarfs all else.*

A year ago Boris had been part of a war-gaming exercise in Tel Aviv where a group of intelligence analysts and military personnel had spent the day role playing the various Israeli responses to learning of an imminent Iranian missile attack on Israel. Boris, admittedly true to form, wanted to question the premise of the whole thing, and the assumptions behind such an attack taking place to begin with. At first he was indulged, and some spirited discussion took place as to whether an Iranian attack was even feasible, until it was pointed out that this was a military scenario they were supposed to be modelling, not a political debating society. At the time Boris had been impressed that his dissent was even tolerated – such questioning while at the KGB would have seen worse postings than the ones he'd had to deal with. At the war games Boris had been placed on 'team Israel' as opposed to 'team Iran' or 'team USA', and it was then that he had come to learn of Israel's development of a long-range drone capable of taking out bunkered targets in deepest Iran. Given his history of working to break the technology boycott of the USSR, he had managed to weasel his way on to this program, especially since a small group of Russians was already involved. He needed to prove that he was useful, not just as an analyst, which is what he'd been reduced to and found frankly boring, but as someone in the field who could be trusted. He loved being in the field.

So he'd produced a risk assessment of the Israeli drone being hijacked by Iran and turned against them. The technology was possible, and the dangers of their own drone being used on their own undeclared nuclear arsenal was worrying. It was a contingency they ought to be planning for, Boris had argued, and he was the man to do it. Boris's strength, which maybe he had oversold, was that he knew people all over Europe and the USA. People that he had cultivated late in the Cold War who were now in positions of some responsibility and keen to 'help' just to see the back of him. In a way the end of the Cold War had created new opportunities for him which he was keen to exploit, and the knock at the window revealed just one such person. He bound up his diary, unlocked the door and let Julian in. It was time to get him more involved in global politics.

'I don't understand,' Julian told him five minutes later. 'Now you want me to create some way of selectively neutralizing the drone? A way of comparing the programmed target coordinates to a hidden set of GPS coordinates? All without it being obvious?'

'Well, you could write a sub-routine called "drone neutralizer", but it would defeat the object, wouldn't it? It's supposed to be a security feature. These things are not infallible.'

'They can be blown up remotely, can't they?'

'Well, firstly they cost millions of dollars, so that's to be avoided if possible. Also, it's not an option if they get into the wrong hands first; they can block the control communication signal if there is one, and at long range even that can't be guaranteed. I need a backup, something that is hardcoded but not detectable if they try to reverse-engineer it.'

'When you say wrong hands, you mean like the Iranians. This is on behalf of the Israelis, then?' Julian asked, as cool as a cucumber, although Boris had expected him to figure that out at some point.

'At least I don't have to explain who I'm working for – you've worked that out,' Boris said, wondering whether the Lebanese partner had blabbed.

'The comments in the code is a giveaway,' Julian said. 'Coders leave signatures, and these were in Hebrew.'

Boris nodded, as if he knew what Julian was talking about. It didn't really matter.

'So, what I also need to do is test the supplier that sub-contracted the work to you. I need to prove, for various reasons, that they are reliable. As you know, they already overstated their abilities, and if we're to use them again we need to make sure they're doing everything possible to maintain the integrity of the stuff they sub-contract.'

'Quality control,' Julian said.

'Exactly, comrade. Quality control. I am the quality controller. I decide who gets contracts and who doesn't. So I want to see if they pick up what you have programmed into the chip.' He watched Julian think about this and took a can of Coke from a cool-box full of melting ice to offer him.

Julian turned it down. 'Why not keep this in-house, within Israel? Why contract it outside?'

'That's easy to answer, comrade. There are certain myths Israel likes to perpetuate, and one of them is that we have unsurpassed technical expertise in Israel. We don't. We often have to use companies outside Israel. But we choose them carefully. They are usually run by people of the right religious and political persuasion.'

'You mean Jews?'

'Not just Jews. Zionist Jews. Pro-Israel. Not all Jews are pro-Israel. Some poor souls have become confused about what is good for them.'

'I thought communists were supposed to be anti-Zionist?'

'You see, Julian, just when I think you are a political ignoramus, you surprise me with these little insights.' He took a swig of Coke which caught the back of his throat and caused him to cough. 'It's a little more complicated than that. The Soviets supported Israel when it was formed. It was the second country to recognize it in 1948, and because of this the Israeli Communist party was tolerated in Israel early on, despite the fact that they were the only organization to give any voice to Palestinians at that time.'

'And your position is what, then?'

Boris was losing patience with the conversation but better to indulge Julian and have him sweet than remind him of the hold he had over him. Persuasion was always better than blackmail.

'Israel is my home now. Russia was my home then. Allegiances are always self-serving. Ideologies do not interest me that much – they never have.'

'So you're a pragmatist. Looking after number one,' Julian said, not without contempt.

'As *you* should be doing,' Boris said, allowing enough warning in his voice, just a little reminder.

'OK, so *if*, and it's a big if, I find a way to do all this, while also bamboozling the company who gave us the work, what then?'

Boris pretended to consider the question seriously. 'There could be some other contract work, although some vetting would be needed, and although I can personally vouch for you, you have a Lebanese partner . . .'

'He's anti-Palestinian and hates Muslims. He's just the ticket, I would have thought. Not Jewish, obviously, but I'm sure you won't hold that against him.' With that Julian opened the door with a view to stepping out, but Boris grabbed his arm and, with the other hand, reached out to close the door.

'I've got eyes on you, Julian, so don't fuck about. Get the work done. You have seven days.'

'Seven days? What if I can't?'

'I have faith in your abilities, Julian. You can't afford to let me down.' Boris let go of him and watched him jump out. After a few minutes he transferred himself to the driver's seat. He needed to go and get supplies, as well as get some air flowing inside the cab. He considered the meeting a success.

TWENTY-FOUR

Sheila never went to Hadfish if she could help it, since it seemed to embarrass Jules to have her there, where he was king in his little world. He liked to compartmentalize things, and although she'd been to the odd company gathering – excruciating affairs with the programmers – she'd never actually visited unannounced. She and Jules socialized with Rami, of course. They'd been doing that before Rami and Jules had even set up Hadfish together, when Julian was still at British Aerospace and would drink to excess to escape the pressures of the job. No, Julian would not like her turning up unannounced, that's for sure. He hated surprises because they threw him off guard. But throwing him off guard was exactly her intention, to try to draw some reaction from him so that he might reveal what was going on. Since he was uncommunicative when coming home late at night, claiming exhaustion (and he did look exhausted), she thought she would try him during the day, offering to take him out for lunch.

After getting reception to ring up to Hadfish so she could gain access, she was alone in the lift and free to examine herself in the mirror. Whether it was the unflattering fluorescent lighting, or that she was tired, or maybe, just maybe, a little dehydrated from too much wine, she didn't like the puffiness she saw around her eyes. She put on sunglasses and that looked better, but then she decided she would look stupid walking into the office with them on, so she removed them and put them on her head.

Since the office manager, Naomi, wasn't at her perch next to the entrance she walked straight over to Julian's office, eliciting no response from the screen-fixated coders, and grateful for the fact that Rami wasn't in his office next door. Julian was talking to a slight woman, her back to Sheila, whose head of shiny black hair, despite being tied up, was a sight to behold and, Sheila imagined, a nightmare to maintain. He was leaning back in his chair, his hands clasped behind his head in that male stance some men unconsciously adopt when trying to exude power. He got up when he saw her and the woman turned round, revealing herself to be young, olive-skinned and very attractive, despite being dressed in an oversized suit which did nothing but disguise her femininity. Julian had recovered enough composure to smile and wave her in, and the woman took a file and smiled at Sheila as she passed, a toothy smile that Sheila couldn't help but respond to.

'Is that the new programmer you've been nurturing?' she asked, smiling, but with just a little snarkiness in her voice.

'Don't be silly, you know very well that's a bloke, Nizar. You can see him hunched over his desk over there, the one with the oversized cans and the ponytail.'

She didn't look round. 'I was joking. Don't tell me – she was hired by Rami,' she said as she sat down opposite.

'No, she just turned up, believe it or not, a replacement for Naomi, who's off sick. She's from the agency.' She watched him write *Ring agency* down on a yellow sticky note.

'I wondered if you wanted to go for lunch. My treat.'

'Really? OK. But it's not such a good time, sweetheart. I'm really snowed under and—'

'That's why I want to talk to you. I've been worried sick about you. To be honest, you're behaving weirdly, like you did when you were at BA Systems just before you quit. Remember?'

He was looking over her shoulder into the open-plan office and she shifted herself to block his view. She knew he wasn't looking at anything in particular out there, it was just that his vision had focused on the middle distance, a place his gaze was often to be found. He re-engaged eye contact.

'I'm worried about you, Julian. I don't know what's going on.'

'Nothing's "going on". I'm just busy, that's all.'

'OK, then. Busy with what?'

'Not that you've ever been interested in my work, but this job here.' He pointed to some electronics on his desk, something connected to his laptop by a cable. It meant nothing to her.

'This is to do with the military contract?' she asked.

'How did you find out about that? I saw all those printouts you left on the table, about the effects of drones. Hardly subtle.'

'That was research for my benefit,' she said. 'I'm sure you already know all about it.'

'How did you find out, though?'

'Does it matter?'

'Yes, it does. It's confidential. Nobody here knows about it except Rami.' He rolled his eyes. 'Fuck, he told Cassandra and she told you.'

'What can I say, Jules – women talk.'

'As does fucking Rami, apparently.'

'The point is,' she said, taking a breath, 'I don't understand why you took it on, since you were so opposed to it.'

'Cassie knows fuck all about what I'm working on.'

Sheila composed herself by looking at the view behind Julian; she could see the arch of King's Cross railway station. She didn't understand why he didn't have his desk facing the window rather than his staff; maybe he felt the need to keep a constant eye on them. He was angry, she could see that. He was pretending to be occupied by something on his screen but his jaw was working beneath his skin.

'Does that mean you don't want to do lunch?'

'It's not that I don't want to,' he said, as if to a child. 'I've just been handed a revised spec and been given another deadline, so I can't.' He was flapping his hands.

'You can't?' She stared at him and was minded to slam his laptop screen closed but he had slumped back in his chair, looking for all the world like he was going to cry. She wondered whether to confront him about whether he was seeing someone else but it wasn't really the right place to do it. She had no evidence at all, just a suspicion that he was seeing someone, that someone else had his confidence, knew him better than she did. *She* wanted his fucking confidence.

'Look, babe, why don't we discuss it this evening?' he said more gently.

She made a face which she hoped conveyed her doubt at this happening.

'I mean it. I'll come home at a reasonable time and we'll eat together.'

'And talk. Properly,' she said, getting up.

'And talk.' He stood up and was going to come round the desk to hug her or peck her on the cheek but she left before he had a chance to. The woman sitting at Naomi's desk looked up at her and smiled as she passed, but Sheila had already put on her sunglasses and didn't engage. Back in the lift she realized that she remained unconvinced by what Jules had told her; he had not explained himself at all and he'd fobbed her off with the promise of further discussion. Two things crossed her mind: the last thing she wanted to become was a nag, and would it have killed him to have lunch with her?

TWENTY-FIVE

I t was the second day Mojgan had been at Hadfish and she was no closer to getting access to what the technical director, Julian Fisher, was working on. She had just watched the blonde woman leave his office. She didn't look at Mojgan, instead hiding behind her glasses after what had seemed like an intense discussion, the sort reserved for people who were intimate. As the woman passed, Mojgan idly wondered why she didn't rejuvenate her fading hair colour. Julian had come in late that morning, looking upset and flustered. He'd gone straight into his office and hooked up the circuit board to his laptop. When she'd seen it on his desk the day before her heart had taken a leap: it was surely what she needed access to. But as he was constantly in his office, peering and tapping at the laptop that was hooked up to the circuit board, it was impossible to have a look. She was also disappointed when she realized that he didn't have a desktop computer. It meant the key-logger was useless in this instance.

Farsheed had been so meagre with the logistics for this mission, yet at the same time so adamant that it was really important, so she had been intoxicated by the excitement, the sense of intimacy sharing a secret between two people can create, especially since they were the only two who knew of her true purpose here. Plus the fact that she had so much autonomy. Just an objective, to be achieved using her own ingenuity. That thought alone gave her a tingle at the base of her neck. A tingle like the one she'd got when she'd put the logger on Julian's partner's computer yesterday. The partner being a good-looking Arab with an easy smile and wandering gaze.

Since establishing that the technical director was her real target, it was disappointing to learn that he was not going to be that easy, and since the key-logger was useless on a laptop, she needed more time and more of her skills. Logging the partner provided some compensation. She'd put it on yesterday while he was still in the office, looking out of the window as he talked on the phone. She'd taken his mail into his office and it had taken five seconds to connect the logger between his keyboard and computer. At least it might yield some information about who they were dealing with, if nothing else, and it would all be added to the sum of knowledge back home; any information about tech companies doing business with Israel was worth noting. In the meantime, she sat at the secretary's desk and trawled her computer for anything interesting, all the while thinking about how she could get access to the laptop Julian Fisher was at that very moment peering intently into.

Mojgan also felt pleased about how she'd handled the black woman whose desk she now sat at. She'd been lucky with her unsecured network, but even password-protected it wouldn't have taken that long to hack it with the software on her netbook.

She'd never had a proper face-to-face conversation with a black person before, not where it hadn't been with a domestic servant. Three days was all she'd asked of her, and all agreed with no violence, or even the threat of violence. That didn't stop her keeping a wary eye on the door, half expecting the woman to walk through it accompanied by the police, having had a crisis of conscience. Judging by her apartment the woman lived alone, and when she'd gained access to her computer through her wireless connection her diary showed no imminent visits arranged, nor was there anything in her calendar apart from a regular fitness class.

The woman's access to the Internet had been too tempting to Mojgan, who – after gleaning what she'd needed to convince the woman to stay at home – had used it to access a secure and encrypted email service she and Farsheed sometimes used for personal communications. She'd left a message for him on the website. He would have to log on to see it, but she was confident that he would at some point, when he got the chance. It was not a work-related form of communication (she never gave him any information that he needed for work using that system), it was simply to let him know how much she missed his physical presence by borrowing the words of the poet Hafez, whom she found less crude than Rumi when it came to describing things of an intimate nature. She knew it would make him smile, her reluctance to call things as they were, but she enjoyed finding ways to describe their lovemaking without calling it what he called it.

Another tingle, but cut short by yet another guy coming up to her with some form, the fourth this morning. They were not subtle, these young men, but they were too shy to make conversation and she took the forms with a smile and placed them in a tray marked 'IN'. The group of six men and two women hunched over the screens looked no different to the ones back home, even down to the headphones and unhealthy snacks they seemed to survive on. One of the programmers, a Middle-Eastern-looking boy with long hair tied back and a wispy beard, came up to her. She half-expected a form, but he was empty handed.

'Let me know if they are bothering you,' he said, tilting his head towards his workmates.

She'd come across this pretend 'I'll protect you from other men' concern before, beloved of young men like this, who laughably proclaimed that she was 'like a sister' to them. She smiled politely and shook her head. 'No, they are no trouble.'

'I'm Nizar,' he said. He had clean hair and a genuine smile.

'Salma,' she said.

'Salma? Where is that from?'

'Turkey,' she said, gambling on the fact that he wasn't Turkish himself.

'Ah. I'm from Syria, originally.'

She nodded non-committally, not wanting to get into a discussion with an Arab about Syria and what was happening there. She knew that her government supported the regime against the so-called rebels; Farsheed's department had even sent someone there to advise on enhancements to software that the government internal security agency used to monitor Internet traffic. There was a chance this guy was sympathetic to the terrorists there.

'Anyway,' he said. 'If you would like to join some of us for lunch, we sometimes go to the greasy spoon down the road.' He scratched his fledgling beard. 'Not just the boys, the girls too.'

'Thanks. But I have much work to do here,' she said, wondering why anyone would want to eat somewhere that was called a greasy spoon. Then she remembered that this Nizar had been in the technical director's office earlier, going over something on his computer, and might be in a position to throw some light on what he was up to. Best not to shut him out completely. She relaxed a bit in her chair and looked up at him, allowing a little warmth into her smile. 'I'll see how I am doing later. It was nice of you to ask,' she said.

He seemed satisfied with this and walked back to his seat. Mojgan went back on to the office manager's computer and continued trying to find as much information as she could relating to the two directors: salaries, home addresses, contact lists, meetings scheduled over the last four weeks. She created a new word-processing document in which she pasted what she believed to be the most useful bits of information. She caught Nizar looking at her from across the room, but he looked away quickly when she did and she concentrated on her task, thinking of Farsheed. A thought, accompanied by the sensation at the base of her neck: Julian Fisher and she were on the same local area network. It could be possible to connect to the circuit board remotely via his laptop, but then the tools she would need to see what was on it were on her netbook, not on the office manager's PC. Perhaps a cable from her netbook, hidden in her bag, discreetly connected to the back of the PC? Think of Farsheed, she told herself; of how proud he'd be that she had shown such resourcefulness.

At the end of her encrypted missive to him she had added a line from Hafez which read, 'Good poetry makes a beautiful naked woman materialize from words.'

TWENTY-SIX

Parking near Naomi's building with a bunch of flowers on the passenger seat beside him at the end of day two of her absence, Julian wasn't so sure it had been a good idea to come. What would he say to her? Maybe he was making too big a deal of it; he was coming to check on her, that's all. As her boss, he was concerned – surely that was appropriate? The fact that he'd heard back from the employment agency and there was some confusion about whether anyone had booked a

temp (once again they were going to get back to him) had also
been a factor. What Boris had said about having 'eyes on you'
had been another. Perhaps those two things amounted to little
more than paranoia. However, Nizar had come into his office
and mentioned, by the by, that Salma, apart from being 'pretty
hot' was also 'pretty mysterious' because if she was Turkish
then he, Nizar, was Pakistani. Julian had dismissed him at the
time (he thought of Nizar as English – his origins hadn't really
interested him) but then it had played on his mind and he had
tried not to stare at the woman for the rest of the afternoon,
waiting for her to leave before he did. Maybe she was Boris's
eyes in Hadfish.

He'd called Naomi as he went to his car and when she hadn't
answered he'd decided on a whim to come and visit her, reckoning on a quick ten minutes before he went home to tell Sheila
whatever he was going to tell her, which he still hadn't worked
out. Maybe this was a kind of displacement activity. When paying
for the flowers he'd found the spa hotel card that Rami had given
him at dinner with Cassie, and had a vague idea that he could
pre-empt any discussion by proposing a weekend there when all
this was over.

He rang Naomi's doorbell. The intercom remained silent so he
rang it again. He listened at the speaker below the buzzers and
turned away, only to see Naomi coming around the corner with
a carton of milk. She hesitated when she saw him, then continued.
It was a long ten seconds for her to reach him.

'What are you doing here?' she said, looking at the flowers
then back at him.

'I thought you were off sick?' He had been holding the flowers
with both hands but let them hang, petals down, by his thigh. If
he could have dropped them without her noticing, he would have.

'Oh, Julian, I'm sorry.' Her face crumpled and he instinctively
reached out for her.

'What's going on?'

She tried to open the door but couldn't see where to put the
key through her tears. He took them from her and got them inside.

In her flat he took the milk from her and went into the small
kitchen where he put the kettle on and found a vase for the

flowers, which he placed on the coffee table in the living room. Naomi had disappeared into the bedroom.

'I'm making some tea,' he shouted into the open door. When he returned with two delicately handled mugs she was on the sofa, red-eyed but dry-cheeked. 'I don't think you take sugar,' he said, offering her a mug and sitting down opposite.

'They're lovely. The flowers. Thank you.'

'OK, Naomi, do you want to tell me what's going on?' She lost her tentative smile and moved her gaze from the flowers to him.

'I've been under a lot of stress lately. Personal stuff . . . Health issues.' She paused and picked at the flowers; they were a mix of things Julian couldn't begin to name.

'You don't have to talk about it, Naomi.'

'No, it's OK.' She looked over his shoulder then into her tea. 'I've been diagnosed with clinical depression. Most days I'm OK, but some days are difficult . . .' She started to tear up and Julian leant across the table and patted her hand.

'I'm sorry, I had no idea, I mean, you always seem so . . . Why didn't you say something? We would have given you some time off, you know that.'

She blew her nose and nodded. 'There's so much stigma attached. You know, people are thinking "why doesn't she just pull herself together", or "sort yourself out". Plus, I don't really want to stay at home on my own, it just makes things worse. I love the job, looking after you. And Rami, of course.'

'But what about family or a . . . friend? I mean, isn't there someone you can go and stay with?'

'My boys have got toddlers – they don't want a depressed, middle-aged woman living with them. And no, there's no fella.'

Julian doubted that she'd even told them about her depression but he wasn't about to get into her relationship with her family. He was no counsellor. 'Are you getting any help? I mean, professional help.'

'You mean a shrink?'

'Well, there's no shame in it,' he said, but held back from telling her was going to see one himself. It wasn't, after all, any of her business.

'I've got antidepressants from my doctor. Still too early to know if they're working.'

'OK, listen, take as much time as you need. The temp seems to know her stuff.'

'Oh, good. I was worried about her. She hasn't . . . done anything, then?' she asked in all seriousness.

'No, of course not, don't worry about her, just concentrate on yourself.'

They drank their tea and Julian looked around the room. She'd tried to make it nice but it was poky at best. He tried to imagine himself living here as a bachelor but the idea of living without Sheila made him panicky. It can't be doing Naomi any good to be cooped up here alone. He had an idea, a way he could help. He fished in his pocket for the hotel business card; Rami had said it was amazing – the treatments alone were bliss. If it was good enough for Rami and Cassie, it was good enough for Naomi, especially if she was getting some one-on-one attention.

'Maybe a change of scene would help.'

'I go and sit in the park down the road.'

'No. I mean you need to get out of here for a few days. I'm going to suggest this hotel and spa in Covent Garden.'

'But—'

'No buts. It's on the company, Naomi, just for two or three nights over the weekend. They give us a special rate,' he said, lying.

'Still, it'll be expensive.'

Julian stood up, feeling determined. 'I insist. They have treatments and stuff like that. You'll be pampered.'

He could see that she was considering it. 'OK. But I'll pay for the treatments.'

Naomi was silent on the journey over and he hadn't pushed her to make conversation, instead automatically putting the radio on to catch the news, only to hear of an explosion in a cinema in Manchester, unknown casualties, the speculation being, inevitably, that it was a terrorist attack. There were also car bombs in Iraq with seventy-three dead, six children killed in Afghanistan after a US bombing raid and the escalating sectarian nature of the civil war in Syria, which had now spread into Lebanon. It was a river of bad news and Julian switched it off before they started the endless conjecture about who might have carried out the Manchester attack if it were a bombing.

'It's coming home,' Naomi said quietly, looking out of the window, and he didn't ask her to elucidate as trying to park in Covent Garden needed his full attention. Ten minutes later and they were entering the small lobby of what looked, on the outside, like a residential house. Julian had called ahead to book a room as Naomi was packing (all they had was a double) and he wanted to go in and pay in advance so she didn't see how much it was. She stood diplomatically to one side as he made the transaction, looking at the leaflet with the available treatments, and Julian wondered whether the receptionist thought they were a couple. Not that it bothered him; Naomi was attractive enough that he wouldn't mind being mistaken for her lover. Conscious of the fact that Sheila was expecting him, he snuck a look at his watch: twenty minutes ago was when he'd been due. He walked Naomi up to the room and watched, smiling, as she politely oohed and aahed at the tasteful decor and quality finish, talking about whether she should have a refloxology or aromatherapy session. Desperate to leave, he hovered at the door, but without any warning she started to sob. It was an instantaneous thing. He had no choice but to go and put his arm around her. She leant in to him, letting it all out like a collapsing dam. Her perfume was pleasantly familiar. Since it was awkward standing up due to their difference in height, he guided her backwards a couple of steps to the bed where they both sat down. He held her like that for a while.

'It's your kindness,' she mumbled. 'It's too much.' She leant in to him some more and he kept holding on.

TWENTY-SEVEN

Arranging to meet outside South Kensington Tube station at this time of day was a mistake, thought Sheila, as a combination of commuters swarming the entrance, desperate to get home and out of the their sticky work clothes, and confused tourists milling about looking for the right way to the Natural History Museum did not make for an easy place to find someone, especially when she didn't know what the private investigator she was meeting looked like. Cassie had assured her that he would recognize her based on Cassie's description. Cassie had been unforthcoming on the matter of what the man had to tell her, saying she didn't know anything herself and that he insisted on talking to her directly. This Sheila took to mean bad news, and after talking to Cassie yesterday evening she would happily have confronted Jules as soon as he'd come home, although she had nothing really to confront him with. She could have just asked him, but then he'd want to know, not unreasonably, why she thought he was seeing someone else, and when she pointed out his behaviour as a reason, he would no doubt put it down to the pressures of work.

It was all academic anyway because she'd fallen asleep on the sofa waiting for Jules to come home, an empty bottle of wine beside her, and woke covered with a blanket which he must have draped over her. He'd been very late again, and she'd stopped bothering with dinner the night after she'd gone in to work and he'd promised to come home early and talk. She looked at the *Evening Standard* headline on the placard outside the station. The story of the terrorist explosion in the Manchester cinema had been retracted; it had turned out to be a leaky gas line leading to a staff kitchen. A minor backlash against some individual Muslims in the street and the firebombing of a mosque had happened in the meantime. Those things couldn't be retracted.

'Mrs Fisher?'

She turned to see a squat bald man in a grey suit standing before her, a whole head shorter, his pate sweaty, probably from the Tube, and he dabbed at it with a tissue as he waited for her to acknowledge him.

'Yes,' she said, looking at his broken nose. She couldn't be bothered to correct both his fallacious assumptions: that she was married to Julian and had taken his name. Perhaps only married people hired private investigators. She wondered what sort of professional would take on a job of watching someone's husband hired by, not the wife, but some friend of hers. Didn't he need permission from the spouse?

He put the tissue away and stuck out a damp hand. 'Rupert. There's a café just round the corner. Shall we?' Without waiting for an answer he set off, and she followed, nervously eyeing the briefcase swinging from his stocky arm.

When they were ensconced opposite each other and had ordered coffee he swung the briefcase on to his knees and clicked it open.

'This is never easy,' he said, taking a large white manila envelope from inside the case. 'Not for me, not for the client.'

Sheila's heart skipped in her chest.

'Just tell me the worst,' she managed to whisper. Rupert waited until the waiter had put down their coffees then leant forward, even though there was nobody in the place since it regrettably didn't sell alcohol and was really the wrong time to be having coffee. Why hadn't she insisted on meeting in a pub?

'The thing is I didn't follow your husband for that long, but I was lucky in the sense that I hit pay dirt early.'

'Pay dirt?'

'Sorry. I mean this could have dragged on but I lucked out, is all I'm saying.' He looked pained – either because he knew he was crap at talking to clients or it was his face of choice for imparting bad news – and opened the envelope. Was he going to produce large glossy pictures and spread them on the table, like in the films? But no, he tantalizingly stopped when the envelope had been opened and looked at her.

'Your husband visited a woman two nights ago and went to her flat. He took flowers. About twenty minutes later they came out of the flat and got into his BMW. She had a small case with her. He drove her to a hotel in town, where they both entered and he was there for fifty-six minutes. He then came out alone and drove home. He paid for a double room.' Rupert paused and recovered his already wet tissue to mop his brow. She hadn't heard him get back that night, she recalled. 'There is every indication of affection between the two of them. They seem quite, erm, close.'

Those words, 'affection', and 'close', seemed to suck all life out of her as well as dim the natural light coming into the room. She could see the investigator mouth something but she had to ask him to repeat himself.

'I was just saying I could carry on, if you like, and establish how, erm, established this relationship is?'

'Who is it?'

He took out a sheet of paper from the envelope, put on some reading glasses and scanned the paper.

'Her name is Naomi Evans. She works at your husband's firm.'

Sheila laughed with relief. 'Are you sure?' He must be mistaken. Naomi, as far as Sheila could recall, was older than she was. Why would he go with an older woman? She could understand, in the way one tried to understand men, that he might be tempted by a younger woman, but this implied something more profound, more than a fling resulting from a mid-life crisis. She couldn't help but think of Naomi's skin colour: was he attracted to her because of it? She watched Rupert check his report and shrug. He looked up, but all she could see was his broken nose.

'It's not unusual for these things to happen in the workplace. Do you know her?' he asked.

'We've met at a couple of company functions, that's all. She's a secretary or something . . .'

Rupert had flipped over the paper to reveal some photos printed on the back. She grabbed it from him and turned it the right way round, holding it away from her face to get focus. The photos were like the photographic story boards she remembered from girlhood magazines, but without the speech balloons and cheesy dialogue. Yes, that was definitely Naomi and Julian in front of a building entrance. He seemed to be opening the door, holding flowers. She looked tearful. A lovers' tiff? Naomi had been off work the day she'd visited Hadfish. Had they fallen out? Maybe she'd broken it off and he was trying to make things up to her, or maybe it was the other way round. In the next one they were emerging from the same doorway, she in a different outfit, looking more composed. He was carrying her case and in the next photo he was opening the car door for her. He'd never opened the car door for Sheila. It was laughable, fucking pathetic. Then, in the next photo, her arm in his, walking into the entrance of a bijou hotel in Covent Garden. A hotel she recognized immediately. There was a shot of them inside, him registering at the desk, she standing to one side, looking nervous. She watched the man opposite talking but her ears were buzzing. She looked unbelieving at the photo of the hotel: it was the same place she'd spent the night a couple of years ago with Rami.

TWENTY-EIGHT

Julian let himself in a few minutes after ten. He put his case in the hall and trudged wearily into the dark kitchen.

'Hello,' said Sheila's disembodied voice, scaring him out of his tiredness. He could see her outline as she moved past the window to the fridge.

'Fuck, Sheila. Why are you in the dark?' His question was answered by the light from the fridge flooding the kitchen and outlining Sheila's form. After days of not even thinking about sex, seeing her like that sparked something in his brain which shot to his groin.

'Do you want something to eat?' she said, addressing the inside of the fridge. 'Or have you already eaten with your girlfriend?'

'What? What the hell are you talking about?' He went to the wall, carnal thoughts banished, and switched on the spotlights recessed into the ceiling. They provided distinct pools of light on the wooden floor, all part of a 'look' they were trying to achieve. Sheila closed the fridge door and leant back against it. She was clutching an open bottle of white wine and had a determined expression on her face.

'What's going on, Sheila? What's this about a girlfriend?'

She walked to the island in the middle of the kitchen, where they used to have breakfast together, and put the bottle down very carefully next to an empty glass already wet with condensation. A large white envelope lay ominously next to the glass.

'Have you been seeing someone else or not?' she asked, pouring wine very deliberately, and it occurred to him that she'd been rehearsing this set-up all evening.

'No, of course not. What's going on?' He went to the cupboard and fetched himself a glass; food would have to wait. He stood on the other side of the island and half-filled his glass from the bottle.

'So can you explain why you've been late every day this week, why you've been so tired' – shaking her head angrily – 'and why you've lost all interest in me?'

'Babe, I've told you, I've been busy at work. I've got this job on that I need to get done.'

'Ah, yes, the so-called drone job.'

'So-called?'

'So there is a drone job?'

'Oh my god. What the hell is this about?'

'Why not just answer the question, Mr Secrets? You love your secrets, don't you? I suppose they give you a feeling of power.'

He sighed and she got herself on to a stool.

'I'm not seeing anyone else,' he said, but she didn't seem to have heard him.

'You're not the only one with secrets, you know.'

'Hurrah, so we all have secrets. I'm not forcing you to reveal any of yours, am I? Are you going to tell me what this is about? Because I'd like to make a sandwich and go to bed. I haven't eaten, with or without my phantom girlfriend.'

'I thought you had ideological objections to working on this kind of thing. I've been looking drones up and it's not pleasant, what they're used for.'

'We're on that again, are we? Yes, I know you've been looking them up, you keep leaving stuff all over the place, as if it's going to make any fucking difference.'

'So just how *did* you overcome your qualms? Was it the money?'

'We've already had this conversation – the company needs the contract. Times are hard, in case you haven't noticed. We're talking about people's jobs, about keeping this house.'

'Don't fucking patronize me. Really.' She glared at him and gulped some wine. He waited for her to resume; she needed to get something off her chest, and best to let her do it in her own time. When *was* the last time they'd had sex? She was right in that he'd had no interest in it recently – since meeting Boris, in fact, who was somehow managing to hold Julian's libido hostage until he completed the work.

'So has Naomi been helping you work late?' She was staring
at him intently.

'Naomi from the office?'

'Yes. How many Naomis do you know?'

'No. She's no coder. Besides, she's off sick. You saw her
replacement, remember.'

'So you haven't seen her outside the office.' He couldn't help
but look away, picking up his drink to cover the fact. At least he
now knew what this was about.

'No, I haven't.' How could she know? He'd told nobody about
about Naomi. Had Sheila happened to see them that night?

'OK, if you're going to lie then there's no point in trying to
have an adult conversation really.'

Julian weighed up the consequences of telling her the truth
and for a moment it seemed like the ideal solution to everything, an opportunity to set the record straight. But then he'd
have to go back to the beginning, to what he'd kept from her
all along.

'Listen, babe, you have to believe me when I say nothing has
happened between me and Naomi. Nothing. I went to see her
because I was worried about her, that's all. In fact, this is
extremely silly and unlike you.'

It was her turn to sigh and she got off the stool and downed
her drink. 'Maybe you can explain this, then.' She slid the envelope across the polished marble top a little too forcefully and it
slid right off and glided to the floor, landing too dramatically for
Julian's liking in a pool of light. He took a step, bending down
to pick it up, a lead weight in his stomach. When he stood up
with it Sheila had left the kitchen and he heard her stomping
upstairs. He opened the envelope and took out the contents.
Details of his movements that night, photos on the back that
looked like . . .

This was fucking bullshit. She'd had him followed and thought
he was having an affair with Naomi. He called out to Sheila; he
had no choice but to explain.

'No need to shout.' She was standing in the hall as he came
out of the kitchen. She was clutching a small suitcase and taking
a summer coat from the coat hanger in the hall. She must have
pre-packed.

'This isn't what it looks like, Sheila,' he said, realizing how utterly hackneyed it sounded.

Sheila hesitated and raised her eyebrows questioningly. 'Tell me what your relationship with her is, then.'

'I don't have a relationship with her.'

'So what were you doing in the photos? You spent nearly an hour in the hotel with her when you'd promised to be home.'

'I was just comforting her.'

Sheila laughed, and it wasn't a joyful sound. 'Really? And you could only do this in a hotel room. A double room. A very expensive hotel, I might add.'

'Look, she's suffering from depression, if you must know. I only discovered that when I went to see her.'

'So you visit all your employees that are off sick and take them to hotels?'

'No, of course not.'

'So why her?'

Julian was stumped. What could he say? That he'd gone to see if she was all right because he was suspicious about the temp who'd taken her place because he'd been warned by his old KGB handler (who by the way was blackmailing him into taking on this drone work) that someone was keeping an eye on him at the office?

'I felt sorry for her, that's all. Come on, Sheila, she's hardly the "younger woman", is she?'

'Who the fuck knows what you need, Jules? Maybe you need a mother figure, someone post-menopausal who'll run you a bath and stroke your head at night. Sex isn't the only way you can be unfaithful – you know that, right?' Sheila opened the front door.

'It's not like that,' he said in a low voice, aware of the neighbours across the way seeing people off. 'Just come in and we can talk about it.'

'Do you confide in her, is that it? Do you put your head in her lap while you unburden yourself? I'd prefer it if you'd just fucked her, to be honest. Do you prefer black women? Am I too pale for you, is that it?'

'Shame on you, Sheila.'

She stepped outside, then paused and turned. 'Why that hotel, out of interest?'

'What?'

'Why did you take her to that specific hotel, of all the hotels in London?'

'I don't know. Rami told me about it. He took Cassie there apparently and said I should take you there, that you'd like it, the treatments . . .' As the words – a simple statement of fact, nothing more – left his mouth, he knew from her face that they were the wrong ones.

She pulled the door gently until it clicked shut. It sounded more terminal to Julian than if she'd slammed it in his face.

TWENTY-NINE

To feel betrayed by two men at the same moment was a cruel stroke of fate and good reason for self-pity. Of course, it was hypocritical of her, but for Rami to take Sheila to a hotel that he subsequently used with the pneumatic Cassie, and then for Jules to take his mother-substitute to the same place, betrayal was exactly what it was. Recalling what she'd said to Julian about him preferring black women made her blush. It wasn't like her. She wheeled her small case down the Fulham Road, gradually becoming conscious that it was quite late, that she was alone on the street, and that she didn't know where she was going. She hailed the next taxi and told him to drive south of the river, just so he had somewhere to go. In the back of the cab she took out her phone and thought about who she could call. Which of her friends would take her in at this hour? They all had kids or were in relationships. Her finger hovered over Cassie's stored mobile number. She looked out at the empty streets and pressed the button. It went straight to voicemail and she hung up, somewhat relieved. On the one hand she felt Cassie bore some responsibility for this mess. Had she not suggested hiring that strange little man she would be blissfully unaware of any of this. She now had some sympathy with the 'turn a blind eye' attitude some women she knew resorted to, but then she was not one of those women who was financially dependent on her husband and having to make life choices based on economic circumstances. Nor was she defined by who she was married to. She and Jules weren't even married, she reminded herself, and at this point she was glad they weren't. The taxi travelled over Chelsea Bridge and she wanted to ask the driver to stop so she could look out over the water, like a forlorn actor in a romantic film, the likes of which Jules was sometimes inexplicably drawn to watching on TV on a Sunday evening. In this scene the taxi driver would wait while she gazed wistfully at the black water and then he would ask her if she was all right and she would pull herself away. She knew full well she was feeling sorry for herself, and besides, the pavement wasn't accessible from the road on this bridge.

She briefly thought about whether she had any right to be upset at Julian's infidelity, when she herself had done the same, in the same fucking hotel. She laughed.

'You all right, miss?' the taxi driver said over his intercom thing.

'Sorry, can we go back north, please.' With a shrug he slowed and swung the cab round in one go to face the other way. She would stay in a hotel for the night, treat herself to somewhere nice but somewhere big and anonymous, like the Marriott on Park Lane, which she recommended to her Russian clients when they were in the UK looking at properties. That meant being back north of the river.

Had Rami meant anything to her? Not really. She could see him now and wonder what it was that ever drew her to him. Embarrassment was the overriding emotion she felt if she ever thought about it. At the time, of course, it was exciting, and she'd fallen for his charm and attention, his interest in her. He'd seemed, she was now ashamed to admit, exotic, foreign, and even two years later, when alone, imagining his brown hands on her white skin created a frisson she used when alone, indulging in her own private fantasy. He'd been a good lover, she'd give him that. Now, though, he seemed a bit of a fool, his exoticism dispelled by his ordinariness. Could she blame Julian for her lapse? She could, if she tried, construct some elaborate pop-psychology rationalization that would pin her actions squarely on his behaviour: his lack of engagement, his constant unexplained symptoms (illness was never attractive in a man), his refusal to have children.

But ultimately it was about her. No one person could provide another with everything they thought they needed, and Rami had inadvertently, due to a technical lapse on her part – over and above the lapse of judgement she had made checking into that hotel – given her the one thing that she had wanted with Julian, and the one thing she couldn't keep afterwards, the thing she'd had to cut short. Something she'd kept from both men.

She'd picked up her phone to call the Marriott and see if they had a room when it started to ring. Sheila smiled with relief when she saw the caller ID and swiped the screen to answer it.

'Cassie.'

'Sheila, I'm sorry I missed your call just now. I've been worried about you but didn't want to call.'

'It was horrible, Cassie.' Her voice cracking, she could say no more.

'Where are you?'

'Taxi,' she managed to say.

'Then you must come to me at once.'

THIRTY

'So, as a fast track into this, Julian, just so we can get the ball rolling, what would you say your greatest fear was?'

Julian shook his head. He'd assumed this meeting would just be a getting-to-know-you session but Dr Truby, or Natasha as she insisted he call her, had got straight to it. Maybe it was a psychological test.

'We're not looking for an answer right now. I'd like you to work on it for next time.' She shifted on the park bench, trying to get more comfortable, and took a slurp through a straw from her small carton of orange juice. They were sitting in Gordon Square, where she'd insisted they meet, since it was, technically speaking, her lunch break and this was supposedly just an exploratory meeting. She'd warned him that her approach was unusual and here she was, asking a question he'd asked himself many times before, albeit unsatisfactorily.

'It helps if you write it down. Draw a triangle on a page and divide it horizontally into five sections. Work your way up from the bottom and rank your fears, with the worst at the pointy end.'

'That's it?' Julian asked, feeling a little disappointed. He was tired after his sleepless night alone, and hungover. He'd been tempted to call Sheila this morning but decided it was best to give her twenty-four hours to cool off, as well as giving himself some time to think of a way to explain everything, or, more accurately, how he might get away with *not* explaining everything. He'd almost cancelled this meeting with the therapist (or was she an analyst?) but then he'd realized it was an opportunity to get some expert input.

'It gives us something to work with, that's all,' she was saying. 'If all it took to make people feel better was to draw a triangle I'd be unable to go on holiday abroad twice a year.'

He looked down at her rainbow-coloured shoes and bare, pale, freckled legs. Her skirt finished just above her knees, something he recalled Sheila saying was a no-no for a woman over forty (which Dr Truby definitely was), even though it had never stopped Sheila showing her legs. 'I don't know about you but I still consider them to be an asset,' Sheila had said, daring him to contradict her. Julian wondered whether he wouldn't have preferred someone a little more frumpy.

'My partner has left me,' he blurted, hoping to shock her out of her faux-friendly professional smugness, but when he heard it said out loud he knew that what he really wanted was some sympathy. 'I mean yesterday, last night, not before I'd made the appointment.'

She seemed disappointingly unfazed by this information. 'I'm sorry to hear that, but in a way it helps focus the issue. It's somewhere to start from.' She turned to look at him; the crow's feet at the corners of her eyes gave her a maternal quality belying the zany shoes, shortish skirt, weird make-up and costume jewellery. Her red hair, probably coloured, was tied back and long enough that the end rested over the back of the bench. Julian wasn't so tired that he was unaware that he was trying to pigeon-hole Dr Truby. She wasn't having any of it, though. Maybe Sheila was right about his need for a maternal figure. His mother had died young, when Julian was just sixteen. His father had been

like most fathers of his generation, kindly but undemonstrative
and incapable of physical affection. After his mother died it was
as if Julian had been tolerated by his father, an uninvited visitor
he was obliged to host in his home, like a child evacuee in the
Second World War. Maybe, he thought, he should be telling
the therapist all this, but she'd said something he'd missed.

'Sorry?'

'I was just asking whether there was someone else?'

'No, no. She thinks there is, but there isn't.'

'Really?'

'Yes, really. I know most people you see are probably having
an affair but I'm not. Neither is she, just for the record.' Although
it had only just occurred to him that she could be. Perhaps all
this nonsense about him seeing Naomi was an exercise in
projection?

'Really?' she asked, and he pointedly gave her a look. She
said nothing and they watched a pigeon approach them specula-
tively, looking for lunchtime crumbs. Julian wanted to kick out
at it but it probably wouldn't have made a good impression.

'I know what you're thinking,' he said.

'Ah, then my husband would love to meet you.'

He smiled.

'So it *is* possible.'

'What is?'

'For you to smile,' she said, smiling herself. 'Now, you were
about to tell me what I was thinking.'

Julian was thrown; she'd disarmed him. He liked her – perhaps
this could work. Maybe he could unburden himself to her. He'd
never done that. Only Boris knew what he'd done, and Boris was
no comfort. It would be such a relief.

'OK, let me have a go,' she said, lowering her voice and
leaning in to him slightly as a couple walked past. 'You think
that I'm thinking that you can't possibly be sure that your wife
isn't seeing someone else.' She sat back and finished her drink,
slurping up the dregs.

He nodded at the pigeon.

'Also, "just for the record", you have no idea the kind of
people I counsel, so don't presume to,' she said mildly.

'You're right, I'm sorry.'

'No worries. So, why does she think you're seeing someone else?'

'She had me followed, and there were some photos that could be . . . misconstrued.' Julian knew how lame this sounded out loud.

'OK, let's park that for the moment. Why do you think she had you followed?'

'Are we having a session, like, right now?' Julian asked.

'No, you're right, but great avoidance technique, by the way.' She put her lunch remains in a bin next to the bench and gathered a large embroidered handbag to her chest. 'Now, do you remember your homework for next time?'

'A triangle with my five top fears,' he said.

She nodded and stood up. 'That's right. Do it for yourself. You're under no obligation to show it to me, of course. So try to be completely honest. Don't overthink it, just do it.' She took out a smart phone and tapped on it. 'Shall we say a week today? We can do it properly next time, in my office. I even have a couch you can lie back on, just like in films.'

Julian nodded and smiled. She walked off, forcing the pigeon to hop out of the way. It then waddled back towards Julian, cocking its head querulously. He checked that Dr Truby had her back to him and kicked out at it. It flew off a small distance unperturbed before approaching him again.

THIRTY-ONE

The inside of the taxi was beginning to smell quite bad. Boris couldn't track down the source, given the increasing mess of newspapers, books and general detritus of living. He'd also started sleeping in it, discovering that an inflatable camping bed fitted width-wise in the back. It felt more secure than going back to his horrible bed and breakfast in Earls Court where the Romanian landlady eyed him with suspicion, like she could somehow sense his responsibility (by association) for the history of her homeland.

Since it was difficult to air the taxi out properly by opening the windows (he couldn't risk it), he'd bought some air freshener, but that had just added another layer of fake pine smell over the top without neutralizing the original. So he'd bought some oranges instead (which happened to be from Israel) and cracked the windows just a fraction to allow a through-draft of air. He sat, an all-in-one-spiral of orange peel on the floor, dripping orange juice on to the open journal on his lap. It was hot, and although the tinted windows helped block out the sun, the black paint of the taxi acted as a heat absorbent, turning the inside into an oven. He needed to drive around a bit with the window open but he was parked outside Hadfish waiting to catch Julian at work, the trouble being that Julian hadn't turned up this morning and Boris had just had a satellite-phone conversation with his boss which hadn't gone terribly well. It looked like he had used up all his partisan Russian sympathy and now they were asking questions about what exactly he was doing in London, apart from 'visiting prostitutes' and developing software. This he was unsurprised by; it was only a matter of time before someone started asking questions. Even the promise of something tangible in the way of intel that they could use was wearing thin; nobody liked a lone operator in this business, he quite understood that. More worrying was the news that they had uncovered a network in Baku which 'they were dealing with'. He'd asked if it was related to what they'd said before about someone coming to London, and was told they didn't know, but the sense Boris got was that they were trying to connect the dots and that he was one of the dots they had drawn a line to. He had to give them something soon, a sweetener, a token of his usefulness. The deadline he had given Julian was just days away now, but other things needed to happen, things over which he had no control. He put aside his diary, in which he had written *Hitlers are everywhere*, and picked up the mobile phone.

Julian answered quickly.

'*Tovarisch*,' Boris said cheerfully. 'How about a visit to the places we used to meet, for old times' sake? Remember that place in Hampstead Heath?'

'What do you want, Boris?' Julian sounded stressed, and he also sounded like he was walking in the street. In other words, not actually working.

'I hope you haven't forgotten our deadline, Julian. May I ask why you are not at work?'

'I don't give a shit about your deadline, Boris.'

'Comrade—'

'I've decided to work at home. Did you put that woman in Hadfish to keep an eye on me?'

'What woman?'

'The one who claims she's Turkish. Is she an Israeli? One of yours?'

'I don't know who you are talking about, but I think a face-to-face would be better than discussing it on the phone.'

'Fuck you and fuck your deadline.'

He hung up. Boris thought about redialling but there would be little point in repeating the conversation while Julian was worked up. He was a nervous type, that was his problem. He remembered when he'd flown him to Moscow from East Berlin for the day in 1988 just to meet with a superior who wanted to thank him for all the work he'd done. He'd taken him to Red Square before they were due to have lunch in the Kremlin and Julian had been terrified that he'd be captured on film by one one of the many camera-wielding tourists streaming from coaches into the square. Boris had had to give him his sunglasses and his fur hat.

Interesting what he'd said about the woman at Hadfish. Could they be that close? But if Julian was now working at home and being difficult, that would be a new obstacle. He may need to up the ante a little.

He dialled a different mobile number.

THIRTY-TWO

After hanging up on Boris, Julian pushed through the lunchtime crowd and tourists to the relative quiet of his car and sat in it to compose himself. He put the seat back and closed his eyes; he'd had so little sleep last night he could easily have dozed off, but found he was too wired after his meeting with the psychiatrist, not to mention Boris harassing him. He felt things were pushing in on him and . . . The phone rang again and he checked to see it wasn't Boris with his fucking withheld number. It was the the employment agency.

The woman on the other end was insistent that Hadfish did not have one of their temps in place. She huffed when he asked her to double-check it on the system and suspected the tapping he heard was just her randomly hitting the keyboard to mollify him. No, she said, it had been a year since Hadfish had taken anyone; had they been using another agency?

Julian hung up. He dug around for the business card of the hotel he'd put Naomi up in and asked to be put through to her room. Reception told him she'd checked out the same evening they'd checked in. She'd insisted his card be refunded for every-thing, and then paid cash for the night they couldn't refund.

'She paid two hundred and whatever it was pounds in cash?'

'Yes, sir, she did.'

He hung up, plugged his phone into the car charger then rang her landline to see if she'd gone home. No answer. He tried her mobile, which just rang endlessly before going to voicemail.

'Hi, Naomi, it's Julian. If you get this please give me a ring. You've checked out of the hotel and I'm concerned.' He didn't tell her about the temp agency; he'd have to confront her with that when he saw her, although he couldn't quite recall if she'd said she'd used the agency.

He decided to get home, just in case Sheila was back. He desperately hoped she was. While driving he ruminated over his call with Boris and wondered if he'd regret talking to him like that. But Boris still needed him, and Julian was starting to seriously think about whether he wouldn't be better off calling his bluff, facing whatever music there was to be faced and, most importantly of all, coming clean to Sheila.

But by the time he'd parked in his street he'd talked himself out of it. He could still finish the job for Boris and avoid damaging things permanently with Sheila. He could get them back to where they were pre-Boris. He just needed to convince her that nothing had happened between him and Naomi, and that should be straightforward to do despite what had taken place at the hotel. There hadn't been any sex – it wasn't anything that affected him and Sheila. What had it been? A moment of tenderness? Comforting a lonely and depressed woman? Perhaps, after what he had just learnt, that thought was misplaced.

Unfortunately Sheila was not at home when he let himself in, nor were there any signs that she'd been there. He tried her mobile but it went straight to voicemail.

'Sheila, it's me. Please call me,' he said. *I want to tell you the truth* is what he nearly added. He hung up and decided to get drunk.

THIRTY-THREE

T he silence in the house on Onslow Square was eerie, even a little creepy. Sheila knew London was out there, but she could easily fool herself into believing she was in the middle of nowhere. She had the urge to strip off and run round the place, screaming at the top of her voice to remove the sense of negativity she was feeling. To rail against the world, and men in particular, would be cathartic. It was definitely hot enough to be naked, but then the Russian-sounding client who'd rung her that morning after she'd left Cassie's (and the first time she'd switched her phone on for two days) would be arriving in five minutes, and she couldn't risk it. Although the thought of him, a complete stranger, finding her in a state of undress made her smile.

She was still a little giddy from staying at Cassie's. There was a sense of unreality about it, an undercurrent of something, like when they'd had lunch, although the night she'd gone round they'd had too many sickly White Russians. Last night, with Cassie out at some PR junket, Sheila had been alone in her small place, going through her wardrobe, covetous of her large selection of lingerie.

She checked her make-up in the downstairs toilet, freshening her lipstick. Then she put on a pair of tights she'd bought on the way over, bare legs not being an option in their current state. She should probably let her assistant, David, know that she was showing the house to this man; she'd agreed this with Jules when he'd fussed about her showing men around on their own. But then Jules was not her bloody keeper. She smiled, imagining his reaction when she told him she'd shared a bed with Cassie. Not that anything had happened, there was literally nowhere else to sleep, and her bed was large enough to accommodate them comfortably. It was more the sense she'd got from Cassie – that if Sheila had been open to it, more could have happened. Maybe she'd just been drunk, maybe she'd misinterpreted Cassie's inno-cent girly sleepover excitement at having Sheila there for something more grown up. But Cassie was no innocent, of that much she was sure. Perhaps she would tell Julian about it later, if they managed to talk; she planned to go home after this, hopefully with the moral strength of a sale behind her. He'd left a couple of messages on her phone and she was willing to listen to what he had to say. Cassie, having helped her uncover his liaison, had tried to comfort her by saying that it most likely meant nothing to him at all. Sex was sometimes just sex, she'd insisted.

The sound of the doorbell echoed around the house and she walked purposely towards the front door, putting her handbag on her overnight case in the the hall, pushing her hair behind her ears with her hands, readying her professional smile.

On the phone he'd sounded like a large man, and he didn't disappoint. Not in the sense that he was overweight, which he probably was, but his frame was big, his chest wide, his shoulders broad. He took up space in the hallway, masculine in the way he stood there without being overtly threatening. Jules was a slight man, in comparison, somewhat tentative when approaching her, but fully engaged when he got there. The moustache on the Russian, who smiled charmingly at her after a quick visual appraisal, was incongruous though; obviously dyed, unlike the hair, and betraying a man who would not grow old gracefully. A man who spent too much time grooming was one to be wary of, both in terms of a marker of too much self-involvement and a lack of confidence. Rami was a bit like that, with his manicures and styled rather than barber-cut hair. She thought all this obsessing over appearance was a bit too, well, feminine for her liking. Sexy was the man who carried what God had given him with pride, a take-it-or-leave-it attitude with good personal hygiene thrown in.

Her potential customer, who was called Boris, could have done with some personal hygiene in the form of deodorant. He was striding forward into the house, opening doors and appraising rooms, leaving a trail of stale sweat for her to follow even though it was not yet noon. His cream linen suit looked like it had been slept in.

'That's the dining room,' she heard herself say in her 'work' voice. 'They had a table in here that could seat twenty, with room to spare.'

The man, whom she now noticed was carrying a small rucksack in one hand and wearing tennis shoes, seemed to be in a hurry. He walked through the kitchen, all but ignoring the hi-tech fixtures, and they ended back in the hall. He glanced upstairs and said, 'Of course, my wife will need to see it, but can we have a quick look upstairs?'

'That is why we're here,' she said. He gestured to the steps, smiling, and a tiny part of her was alerted. Was it playfulness in his eyes? However, she was not going to be churlish by insisting he go first. He was either being chivalrous or wanted to ogle her behind. Both were the flip side of the same sexist coin, as far as she was concerned. But if this guy wanted to look at her bottom as he followed her upstairs she wasn't going to make a big thing of it, not with the huge commission the sale of this house would yield. But as she took the steps she remembered, due to the tightness she could feel round her buttocks, that she was wearing a suit she'd borrowed from Cassie. She hadn't taken any work clothes when she'd left home, and hadn't had time to go back before coming here, although the idea of finding Julian moping around the house had also been a deterrent. The only thing less appealing than a leering man was a moping man. Fortunately, although Cassie and she shared a waist size, Cassie had wider hips and more of a bottom, so the skirt was loose enough not to be too tight as she walked up. It was, however, a lot shorter; Sheila hadn't worn anything this short for fifteen years. Making it to the top of the stairs, she stopped and turned. Boris, seemingly unaware of her sartorial insecurities, was panting as he reached the landing.

'Russian cigarettes,' he said, explaining his laboured breathing. He paused as she stood at the top. 'Is there a bathroom up here?'

She nodded and pointed to the door directly opposite the stairs, behind which was a small cloakroom with no window. It was not a huge selling point for the house, although it was nicely tiled in black and white on the floor and all the way up the walls, but there were three other bathrooms in the place so he might as well see the worst first and get it over with. He went in, and, without closing the door, ran some water in the small sink and splashed it on his face. She turned away as he discovered there was no towel and wiped his big hands on the back of his trousers. No need to embarrass the guy, although he did not strike her as the sort to care what people thought. A lot of these got-rich-quick Russians were like that. Their children, who went to expensive private schools and had therefore picked up the nuances of the English class system, were often visibly horrified by their parents' uncouth behaviour when they accompanied them.

'What is this, please?' the Russian said. She turned. He was still in the cloakroom and pointing to something above the door inside. They always picked up on some small thing she hadn't noticed. Was it a tiny speck of mould due to the fact the room was windowless? She put on her smile and at the entrance to the room stood to one side so he could come out and she take his place; no way was she was squeezing in there with him. He understood and came out.

'Have a look,' he said.

She stepped inside and turned round just as the heavy door closed gently on her. She heard the key turn before she had time to register what was going on. For some unfathomable reason she looked at the wall above the door where he had been pointing but she could see nothing but shiny black and white tiles.

THIRTY-FOUR

The sound was inside his head, a loud two-tone bell inside his head. Stirring, finding himself on the sofa in his underwear, he heard the sound again. A doorbell. His doorbell. It couldn't be Sheila; she had a key. He pulled himself upright, causing a surge of nausea. An empty bottle of wine sat accusingly on the coffee table, an amount he was not used to handling. The laptop was open beside it, having gone to sleep itself some hours ago. The cable that connected it to the circuit board was there but he couldn't see the board. Had he moved it? Maybe he'd spilled wine on it. The doorbell sounded again and he looked for his trousers. They were crumpled up on the arm of the sofa, along with his shirt. It had been unbearably hot last night, now he remembered. A vibrating noise from the table. His phone. Please let it be Sheila. No, it was bloody Rami. Had he missed a meeting? He hadn't been at work the last couple of days, supposedly working at home, but the truth was he just couldn't concentrate. He had, in fact, come up with a theoretical solution to Boris's little requirement last night, but he'd done nothing about it. He didn't really care. He picked up the phone, which was sitting on a piece of paper, on which he had drawn his triangle divided into five layers. He'd written *dying* in the smallest top segment and *flying* in the bottom. 'Hey man, I'm outside your front door. Are you in there?'

Julian pocketed his 'triangle of fears', revealing the circuit board underneath. He hopped to the door, pulling up his trousers. Rami, unusually for him, was unshaven and looked as worn as Julian felt.

'May I come in?'

Julian tilted his head and held the door open by way of answer before following Rami into the living room.

'I see you've been busy getting drunk. And that,' pointing at the circuit board, 'wasn't supposed to leave the office.'

'Did I miss a meeting or something, or are you just here to check on me?'

'No, I heard about you and Sheila.'

Julian wanted to ask how he'd come about this information but his mouth was dry.

Rami, unusually attuned to his condition, went into the kitchen and came back with a glass of water. 'Why don't I make some coffee while you shower? You look like shit.' Without waiting for an answer he headed into the kitchen. Julian dragged himself upstairs.

Twenty minutes and two painkillers later, Julian came down to find Rami sitting at the kitchen island, scrolling through something on his Blackberry, probably his Facebook or Twitter feed. With his free hand he pushed a cup of coffee over the counter.

'Have you seen Sheila then?' Julian asked, inhaling the aroma.

Rami shook his head vigorously. 'No, of course not. I saw Cassie last night. She spent the last couple of nights at hers,' Rami said, looking over his reading glasses at Julian. At least that answered one of Julian's questions. 'I take it she didn't call you last night, given your state this morning.'

Julian shook his head. He'd tried to ring Sheila again last night, a few hours after leaving her the earlier message and exactly twenty-four hours after her leaving home, but it had gone straight to voicemail again. By then he hadn't been capable of leaving a sober-sounding message or one where he didn't sound sorry for himself. Also, he wasn't sure what he would have said; he'd decided, after much alcohol, that he didn't really feel he had anything to apologise for, except for being untrue to her ever since he'd known her, and that wasn't something he was going to do over the phone. This misunderstanding, of course, was merely a symptom of his withholding, he knew that. Like the stomach aches and the panic attacks. And yet he was still thinking about how he could fix it without going back to the original lie of omission.

'So did Cassie tell you what happened?' he asked Rami, who'd put his phone away.

'She just said you'd been seeing someone else. Is that true?' He sipped his coffee and looked at Julian expectantly but when Julian didn't answer said, 'If you want to talk about it . . .'

Julian sat down. 'There's no one else.' Julian decided against telling Rami about Naomi and her depression, even though he may already have heard the details through Cassie, who liked to gossip. Or maybe Sheila had kept the details to herself. 'Have you been to the office today?'

'No, I came straight here. Why?'

'That woman, who filled in for Naomi, what was her name . . .'

'Salma.'

'Yes, Salma. Was she in yesterday?'

'Yes, she was. Why do you ask? Oh my God, she's not the other woman, is she? She hasn't even been there long.'

Julian put up his hand. 'Stop right there, Rami, before your imagination gets the better of you.'

Rami held up his hands in surrender. 'OK, but if you were going to choose someone to—'

'There wasn't anybody, can we establish that, for fuck's sake. This whole thing has got out of hand and to be honest I think Sheila's being a little childish.'

'OK, man, calm down.'

Julian remembered to breathe and studied Rami. He looked tired. He'd known him for a long time but how much did he really know him? OK, best not go down that path. He shook his head in an effort to clear it. 'You told me that Naomi had arranged her as a replacement.'

Rami shrugged. 'I probably assumed she had – I mean, she's super efficient like that.' That was true enough.

'So you weren't involved in hiring her? The company we subcontracted this bloody job from didn't tell you to hire her?'

'OK, Jules, you're starting to worry me. I'm sure she came from the agency. Like I said, Naomi must have sorted it out.'

Julian shook his head. 'The agency knows nothing about her, I checked. That's why I'm asking you. It's a reasonable question if you think about it. You were keen, indeed very keen, for me to take the job. You have been very cagey about the details. In fact, I still don't know the name of the company that approached you. Maybe this woman was sent in to keep an eye on things, make sure the job was being done?'

Rami sat there staring at him, as if he were mad.

'Maybe, because this is stuff that is eventually going to end up in government hands, a government agency has an interest in it.'

'Listen, man, you've been working too hard. You—'

'Don't fucking bullshit me, Rami. This whole thing stank from the start.'

Rami stood up and put his hands on the counter. His nails were bitten down; usually they were perfectly filed.

'Listen to yourself, Julian. Your woman, your partner of almost thirty years has left you and you're ranting about some conspiracy theory. You've got your fucking priorities wrong. Don't you even care about getting Sheila back?'

'Don't ask stupid questions, Rami. Anyway, it's a personal thing.'

'It stopped being personal when she became friends with Cassie and went to stay with her.'

Julian snorted. 'So it impacts on your sex life and you get concerned? And Cassie and Sheila are friends? Really? I mean, it's not like they have a lot in common, is it?'

Rami stood up straight. 'What's that supposed to mean?'

Julian shrugged. Maybe he'd gone too far. 'Nothing. I mean there's an age difference, that's all . . .' But Rami was already walking to the door. He stopped when he got there and turned.

'I never thought I'd say this, right, but have you considered that it's you and Sheila that don't have a lot in common? You don't know how lucky you are to have someone like her, she's a lovely and . . . vibrant woman. Maybe you should pay her more attention.'

He stood in a challenging stance and Julian was unable to say anything, such was his surprise. Had he just said Sheila was vibrant? What did he know about maintaing a long-term relationship? But Rami visibly relaxed, softened his stance and attempted a familiar conciliatory grin. Julian's desire to tell him to mind his own fucking business dissipated.

'Look, I'm sorry,' Rami said gently. 'We're all under pressure here.'

Julian nodded, failing to see how Rami was under pressure.

'But maybe the best thing would be for you to concentrate on the work. Use it as a distraction. She'll be back, trust me.'

'I just want to know that she's all right, that's all,' Julian said, hating the break in his voice.

Rami stepped up to him and put his hands on Julian's upper arms. 'I'm sure she's fine. Why don't I get Cassie to call her, then at least you'll know she's OK? She'll speak to Cassie.'

Julian nodded.

'Good. I'll call you as soon as I hear something. Just focus on the work, right? We need to get it done. Then you can concentrate on sorting things out with Sheila.'

'Don't you get it? I don't really care about the job. Until I sort things out with Sheila I can't concentrate.'

Rami dug his fingers into Julian's arms. 'Listen to me, Julian. You've got to finish it. It's important,' Rami said with new urgency. 'Please tell me you'll try to focus.'

Julian shook himself from Rami's grip. 'Stop it. As soon as I've sorted things with Sheila, I'll finish it,' he said.

He heard Rami leave and found himself covered in sweat. He was struggling to take in air. His heart pounded and something was pressing down on his chest. He was in no doubt that he was about to die, and what terrified him was that he was going to be alone when it happened.

THIRTY-FIVE

B oris had decided that once it was dark he would move his things, not that there were many of them, from his taxi into the house on Onslow Square. It would be ideal as his new base. Sheila had been considerate enough to remove her jacket and leave it with her handbag on a small suitcase in the hall. He had assumed that any keys or mobile phone would be in them, since anything in her skirt pockets would have been obvious; he could make out the high cut of her underwear as he'd climbed the stairs behind her. He had her jacket and bags with him now, and, finding a new model mobile phone, switched off in a jacket pocket, he emptied her handbag on to the floor. A wallet, with some money, cards and a faded picture of Julian in which he had more hair. He'd been handsome back then, if a bit of a loner, which is why Boris, observing him at those dreary Socialist Workers Party meetings, had known he was suitable material, not to mention the attraction of his technical training. Boris looked at the other items on the floor. Two sets of keys: one with the current address on them, the other he assumed were her house keys. Lipstick, moisturizer, a hair brush containing some of Sheila's hair, a packet of half-consumed painkillers, a battered tampon in its paper wrapper which had gathered lint, perhaps kept for emergencies, an old shopping list with *wine*, *butter* and *milk* crossed out, a leaflet giving guidance on setting up a charity, an identity badge for the Chelsea and Westminster Foundation Trust NHS

Hospital labelled 'Volunteer' with a photo that didn't do her justice, and finally, a bottle of water, a third empty. He put all these items, apart from the water, back in the handbag and opened her suitcase. He could hear nothing from upstairs; the doors and walls here were solid, and the bathroom did not adjoin the house next door, so there was no risk of being heard by the neighbours even if she did kick up a fuss. She would be fine for now, although he needed to go shopping. He opened her overnight case. Just some jeans, T-shirt, used underwear and a nightgown. There was also a washbag that included more make-up, an electric toothbrush and toothpaste. He removed some nail scissors and a nail file.

He went upstairs with his rucksack, which he put down outside the bathroom door, and spoke into where the door met the frame. 'Please stand back from the door.' He heard movement and unlocked the door. He then opened it and looked in. She looked wary rather than terrified. 'I'm not going to hurt you,' he said.

'What do you want?' she asked, trying to appear firm. If she was scared, and she ought to be, she was hiding it well.

'Nothing. Well, not from you, anyway,' he said by way of reassurance. 'I'm going out for an hour or two. When I return I'll explain. You shouldn't be here more than twenty-four hours.'

'You can't keep me here. It's kidnapping.'

'We'll talk when I get back.'

She hung her head and put her hands to her face, making a sobbing noise. 'Please,' she said softly, her voice now whiny.

The seriousness of what was happening was perhaps beginning to dawn on her, he thought. He was stepping back in order to close the door with his right hand when she sprang. One second she was looking like she was about to cry, the next she was screaming and rushing at him, using her nails like claws at his face. He instinctively stepped back and stumbled, which gave her some space on his weaker left side, but she couldn't move fast in that skirt. As she rushed past him, heading for the top of the stairs, he managed to get his left fist to her shoulder which made her veer into the wall, slowing her up. Swivelling, he got to her as she reached the stairs, grabbing her left elbow as her arm stretched behind her mid-stride. His grip and her forward momentum caused her to swing ungracefully in an arc to her left, her face meeting the egg-shaped wooden ornament on the newel at the top of the stairs. She groaned and fell to her knees. Keeping hold of her left arm, Boris twisted it behind her.

'Bastard,' she said, muffled with pain.

'Get up.'

'I'm hurt.'

He checked her face. Her nose was bleeding as well as a cut above her left eye. She had the kind of skin that would bruise colourfully but she hadn't been knocked unconscious and the cut wasn't bleeding badly.

'You'll live. Get up.' He motivated her with a twist of her arm and she stood, wobbling. He propelled her into the cloakroom, picking up his rucksack. This time he locked them both in and found the duct tape, which he'd hoped he wouldn't have to use, in his rucksack. Stupid woman. He was angry that this had happened. But maybe he'd be able to turn the event to his advantage.

THIRTY-SIX

'What's with the beard?' Mojgan heard Rami Haddad ask the Syrian boy, Nizar, who had stopped Rami as he was passing to ask whether Julian would be in today, saving her the trouble of trying to find out herself. Rami had told him Julian was working at home. So much for getting network access to the circuit board – she had downloaded the requisite software last night on to her netbook ready to have a crack at it today. It was now going to have to be a hands-on job. That's when Rami started quizzing Nizar.

'Are you religious?' Rami was asking, too loud, obviously wanting everyone to hear him.

'What's that got to do with anything? I'm just growing a beard. It's not against company policy, is it?'

'Not if it's not for religious purposes, no. Religious beards are not allowed.'

Nizar looked uncomfortable, as if he wasn't sure whether the boss was joking or not. Mojgan couldn't tell either, until Rami threw her a wink. Unfortunately this was for her benefit – he actually thought she would be impressed with a display of bullying.

'And the ponytail, is that a religious ponytail? Because if so it will need to come off too.'

Nizar was trying to edge round Rami but he stopped him and unbuttoned his shirt. 'It's OK,' he said, pulling out a gold cross. 'I have a symbol of my religion too, but I keep it hidden. It's not on display for everyone to see.' He laughed and Nizar grinned stupidly before moving back to his workstation. Rami came over to Mojgan's desk, his shirt still half undone, the hair on his chest poking out.

'I like to have some banter with the staff,' he said, taking his time to do up his shirt. She didn't know the meaning of the word 'banter', but his breath smelled of alcohol even though it was only lunchtime. 'So, have you been with the agency long?' he asked her.

Mojgan shook her head, thinking, *What agency?* Surely he didn't mean the intelligence agency. She could feel the sweat pricking at the back of her neck, under her hair.

'What, three months, a year?'

'I'm not with an agency.'

'So how did you get this job?'

It dawned on her what he was talking about; he meant an employment agency. Naomi had mentioned something about that.

'Naomi contacted me directly for this job,' she said.

'You're a friend of hers?'

'Friend of a friend.'

'A friend of a friend. So, did Naomi tell you how much you would be paid?' he asked.

Was he trying to catch her out, or was this his idea of flirting?

'No, she said you would sort it out.'

He finished buttoning his shirt but the little gold cross was swinging free as he leant over her.

'Of course I'll sort it out. Come into my office and I'll sort it out right away. No need to be shy. Come.' He walked off and she picked up a pad and pen, just for something to hold so her hands wouldn't shake. Inside his office he closed the door behind her and went to his desk.

'Do I have to pay you more than Naomi because you are pretty?' he asked, with that stupid grin. She felt herself redden and fixed a smile. She hated it when men made compliments about her. She sat in the chair next to his desk, hunching into herself. She was desperate to leave but needed the logger from his computer.

'You *are* shy.' His phone rang and he lifted a finger as if to put her on pause. He took his call at the desk, gesticulating as he talked about some bid process. She glanced into the open-plan office, then, as she watched him looking out of the window, felt for the keyboard cable at the back of the desk and followed it with her fingers until she reached the key-logger at the computer. He turned and reached down for his keyboard. She hesitated. He tapped something in, the phone wedged between his head and shoulder. He read out a number from the screen. She pulled the key-logger out of the computer then removed it from the keyboard cable. The cable dropped behind the desk, making a clunking noise as it hit the desk leg. He turned as she pocketed the logger. She'd have to leave his keyboard unplugged. She stood up, seeing his quizzical look, him asking for a minute with his finger again. She shook her head and left the office, picking up her bag without stopping and heading for the exit. In the lift down to the lobby she took deep breaths and wondered how long it would be before he worked out why his keyboard wasn't working.

When the lift opened in the lobby she was face to face with a blonde woman in a short red summer dress that showed her contours and exposed the deep valley between her breasts. She was close enough that Mojgan could smell the woman's sickly perfume. Why was this woman going around displaying herself like this? Was she trying to attract a husband? The morality police in Tehran would throw a blanket over this one and whisk her down to the police station as fast their minivan would allow. At least she knew how to colour her hair properly, unlike Julian's wife. Mojgan, who could see two mini versions of herself in the woman's large sunglasses, pushed by her and departed Hadfish forever.

THIRTY-SEVEN

The Russian had tried to leave the light on in the small bathroom. It hadn't worked, but even if she'd owned a watch it would have been impossible to tell the time since her hands were bound behind her with tape. He'd been gone for at least a couple of hours, although her judgement of the passage of time was impaired by the lack of light. It was pitch black at first, then some light had started to filter through an extractor fan in one corner near the ceiling. But it had faded.

Her arms stiff, her eye throbbing and desperate for a pee, she managed to get herself from the floor on to her knees, then, gradually, she pulled up her skirt at the back, now grateful that she was wearing Cassie's short skirt since it would otherwise have been impossible. Pulling down her tights and underwear proved a more awkward challenge, and progress was painfully slow, every movement a torture to her bursting bladder. Eventually, with the relevant bit exposed, she shifted herself on to the toilet, relieving herself with a satisfied groan. Afterwards she sat there, exhausted at her efforts, breathing through her nose because of the tape around her mouth. Hearing Boris come in the front door, she started to inwardly laugh at her own predicament and the embarrassment of him seeing her like this. The irony of worrying about him seeing her on the toilet when, for all she knew, he planned to rape and kill her was not lost on her. If she came out of this Jules would have 'I told you so' tattooed on his bloody forehead. She stood and tried to pull up her underwear and tights, but this proved more difficult than pulling them down. She managed at least to pull the skirt down over the bunched mess of it all, to flush and to put the toilet cover down, which she then used as a seat. He didn't seem like a rapist, but then rapists came in all shapes and sizes. She tried to reassure herself that most rapists were people you knew; they didn't usually go to all this effort except in lurid TV crime dramas. But if not a rapist, what was he?

She listened to see whether she could hear him. The doors in the house were solid, but the downstairs floor had bare floorboards and there were echoes coming up the staircase, as if he was pulling something in from outside. She tried to contain her imagination. Her left eye was half closed. She could hear him lumbering up the stairs, dragging something behind him, then he went back down again. About ten minutes later he came back up, and she heard him breathing heavily from the climb. The key turned in the lock. She tried again to pull the skirt down as best she could and look dignified; the last thing she wanted to do was give the impression she was helpless or scared. The door opened and she squinted as light from a camping lantern flooded the room. He placed it on the floor.

'The electricity has been cut off,' he said. Yes, that would happen about now, she realized, between residents. He reached outside the room and to her surprise produced a bottle of wine, two plastic cups and a paper plate of supermarket-bought sandwiches. He put these on the floor too before bringing in his rucksack and locking the door behind them. She tried not be intimidated by his physical presence in the small space. At least he smelled fresher than he had earlier in the day. He took a smartphone that looked like hers from his pocket, fiddled with it, his eyebrows furrowed, then pointed it at her face for several seconds before switching it off and pocketing it. This suggested to her that some purpose existed to all this. But maybe he was just going to send it to his friends, and now he was just waiting for them to arrive. She shouted *stop* in her head, forcing herself to focus on the facts, to read his expression. He reached out and yanked the tape from her mouth; like a brutal version of the waxing she sometimes subjected herself to at the beauty salon, but she tried not to show the pain.

'I'm going to untie you. Please don't try any stupidity again.' She looked at him with no emotion. He took a penknife from his pocket and held it up expectantly. She half turned and offered her hands. He cut through the tape and she pulled it from her wrists, showing him the results. He ignored them, pouring wine and holding out a cup.

'Water,' she managed, hoarsely.

'Of course.' He put the wine down and produced her bottle of water from his rucksack. She drank greedily.

'I didn't want to do that, but I had no choice. I apologise.'

She could smell the wine but ignored the once-again proffered cup, tentatively feeling her face instead.

'Have a drink, please, and I will explain what is going on, within limits.'

She was still thirsty but knew the wine would calm her down and help her think. It wasn't the time to practice abstinence.

She took it then halted, worried that it was drugged. Noticing her hesitation, he rolled his eyes and took the cup from her, swigging from it and and passing it back.

'It's a Chilean Shiraz,' he said. She took it, drinking deeply, not caring if she looked desperate. He nodded in approval and lowered himself into a sitting position on the floor, his back against the door, pouring himself a cup. She watched him carefully. He looked like he was going to make a toast then decided against it, instead taking a drink and wiping his moustache with his free hand. His fingers were big; she could still feel his grip on her elbow.

'So what's going on? What's all this about?' The wine had given her a bit of Dutch courage, and she was somewhat re-assured by his laid-back attitude.

'Are you starting a charity?'

'What?' He must have gone through her bag.

'Is it for animals? The English love animals, more than people, and who can blame them.'

She shook her head.

'OK, don't tell me. Let me guess.' He studied her like a stage psychic trying to discern the name of a pet from an audience volunteer. She touched the bruise over her eye. She wanted to get up and look at herself in the mirror. He pulled a small first-aid kit from his rucksack. 'Here, you can clean it up later but it's just a small cut and a large bruise.' He put his palm to his chest. 'I'm really sorry it happened. I hate to see a woman's face bruised. It's not right.'

'But tying a woman up is OK?'

'Tying you up was necessary, in order to make the world a safer place. Eat something. I hope you are not one of these silly vegetarian women. It's chicken.'

She took a sandwich just to keep him talking.

'Aha! Is it something to do with the environment, your charity?'

'No. What do you mean, to make the world a safer place?'

'I mean I need Julian to do something for me that will make the world a safer place.'

'The drone software,' she said, enjoying the surprise on his face.

'Ah, so he's talked to you about it.'

'No, not really. He was reluctant to do the work.'

'Yes, he was, and I,' he said proudly, as if showing off his powers of persuasion, 'convinced him otherwise. But most recently he seems to have lost all interest. You are here, let us say, to focus his mind.'

She took a bite of her sandwich, finding it tasteless but discovering how hungry she was. She chewed and thought about what to say.

'If he didn't tell you about the work, who did?' he asked her.

'Nobody. I just put two and two together.'

'Perhaps from his partner, the Lebanese?'

She shook her head.

'Then from his girlfriend, perhaps. He is, what do you call it, loose-mouthed.'

'Loose-tongued.'

'Yes, loose-tongued. The opposite of Julian, he has always been secretive,' Boris said.

She looked at him with renewed interest. 'Always? How long have you known Julian?'

He smiled. 'From before you both met,' he said. 'I knew of you from the start.'

She tried to process this. 'From university, then?'

He nodded, seemingly distracted with thought. 'Your father was a diplomat, wasn't he? He spent a few months in Moscow?'

'Yes, but—'

'I had you checked out, you see.' He was smiling mischievously.

'Checked out?'

'Yes. I couldn't have my Julian hooking up with any woman. You were perfect, though, just the right sort.'

'The right sort? The right sort for what?'

'My dear, you must refrain from repeating everything I say. I know this comes as a surprise to you, and on one level I admire Julian for not spilling the beans all these years. I'm not sure I could have kept it from you for that long. I would like to tell you all about it.' Sheila caught herself leaning forward, engrossed by what this man was saying. She reached for the bottle but he got there first. 'Allow me.' He poured wine and moved the bottle beside him. He must have thought she wanted to use it as a weapon, but nothing had been further from her mind. He looked at his watch and got up.

'Where are you going?'

He laughed, a deep and natural sound. 'I've enjoyed our little chat, too, but I need to make some phone calls. I promise to be back in a few hours.'

'But you haven't told me anything. What did Julian keep from me? Did Julian work for you at British Aerospace?'

He shook his head. 'Later, my dear. Now, if I leave you untied will you behave?'

She nodded.

'No shouting or banging?' Banging, she hadn't thought of banging. She nodded, but he caught her glancing at the pipes and sighed.

'Banging is pointless,' he said, 'because this room is in the middle of the house. But it will annoy me and that is not a good idea, as you have seen' – he pointed to her eye – 'and if you want to know about Julian, then you'll keep quiet tonight. If you make a noise, I'll have to restrain you again, and I'll tell you nothing.'

He unlocked the door while facing her, then opened it, dragging in a rolled-up camping mattress. He also threw in her washbag, which he must have taken from her overnight case. He topped up her cup with wine then took the bottle. 'Remember to drink water,' he said, pointing at the sink. He backed out of the room, began to close the door then stopped. 'Is it for children?'

'Is what for children?'

'The charity you are setting up. Is it for children with cancer? People love to help children with cancer.'

'Yes, it's for children. Afghani children injured by cluster

bombs. They need artificial limbs, and people who can fit them.'
He looked surprised and studied her for a moment.

'Why? I mean, why Afghanistan?'

She wondered why the hell she was having this conversation
with this person, but part of her had a need to explain it.

'I don't know really. It was just coincidence that it was Afghan
children, they could have been Iraqi, Syrian, whatever. But I
needed to . . . engage somehow, with the wider world. It's my
way of dealing with the mess that we created in the first place.
It's our mess. Does that make sense?'

He nodded, as if what she'd said wasn't stupid. 'It makes
perfect sense. Unfortunately, charity is not the answer, it's just
like giving aspirin for something like, I don't know, malaria; it
doesn't deal with the mosquitos that spread the disease. If Julian
cares about you, which I'm sure he does, we'll hopefully get a
chance to talk again in the morning, before you go. I will leave
the light.'

She had to restrain herself from saying goodnight to her
kidnapper and heard the key turn in the lock. As she listened to
his heavy footfall on the stairs she rummaged in her washbag to
find he'd removed the nail scissors and file. She sat back, her
brain buzzing with what he'd said about Julian. Maybe, just
maybe, she'd had him all wrong.

THIRTY-EIGHT

Julian's triangle of fears was gradually taking shape. At first
he'd thought it would be too easy to fill out but then he'd
struggled after putting *dying* at the top of the triangle and *flying*
at the bottom, with *ill health* somewhere in the middle. Then he
worried that placing *dying* at the top would only show how self-
absorbed and lacking in imagination he was; after all, didn't
everyone having a fear of dying? With Sheila gone he'd become
acutely aware that *being alone* ought to go on the list, but then
he was quite happy being on his own for periods so he crossed
that out and put *being unattached*, then moved it under *dying*.

But maybe his fear of dying was not a fear of death but actually a fear of dying without having achieved anything in his life, or even, he thought, *belonging* to anything. It was the real reason he had attended those Socialist Workers Party meetings all those years ago, to belong to something that seemed worthwhile, but then Boris had come along (he'd never really understood what Boris was doing at Trotskyist party meetings), claiming to offer something better to belong to, something that he said would actually make a difference rather than be a talking shop. But all he'd ended up belonging to was Boris – and only Boris – and he'd become even more isolated. He didn't even have a circle of friends he could claim to belong to. Who were his real friends? Who could he go to with his current problem? The group he and Sheila had considered their friends had gradually shrunk as they had kids and made new friends with other people with kids. Maybe he and Sheila should have had children, but he'd been reluctant, and he couldn't even remember, in his freshly inebriated state, why he hadn't wanted them. Maybe he'd felt he was just incapable of that sort of nurture or responsibility. She'd mentioned children on and off for a while then suddenly stopped mentioning them, which was somehow worse, and now it was too late. They were both too old.

And what about Rami? He could have come clean to him yesterday about the whole mess. He'd known him for years, but what really bound them together was the business, not much else, and the business necessarily took precedence over any real friendship. Rami had annoyed him yesterday with what he'd said about Sheila. But maybe Rami, in his cack-handed way, was right about Julian not appreciating her and even about them not having that much in common, after all. But then having things in common was not, in itself, enough of a bond. Why, for instance, had Sheila gone to Cassie, with whom she had nothing in common, and not one of the other people they called friends? Probably, he guessed, for that very reason, because the idea of telling her 'friends' that he was cheating on her would be too difficult. Although the very word 'cheating' was so lacking in meaning and loaded with a conditioned implication of 'ultimate betrayal' that he couldn't really take it seriously. His feelings for Sheila hadn't changed, but maybe his expression of them had.

He put his head in his hands, mentally exhausted. Don't overthink it, the analyst had said. He emitted a laugh that sounded like a cough and thought about refreshing his drink. He checked his phone. Nothing. He could try ringing her again but her phone was dead; she probably hadn't taken her charger or had switched it off. He could try Rami, to see if Cassie had spoken to her, but he would have rung if he'd heard anything. Sheila would surely realize, given time to think, that he wouldn't lie to her about something as serious as this, especially after being confronted with so-called evidence. But then he had lied to her, even if it was a lie of omission. Lied to her for years because he was afraid she'd leave if he told the truth.

He topped up his whisky and made his way carefully back to the sofa where he slumped into the hollow he'd created. He jumped when his phone beeped with a message. He snatched at it, hoping, praying, checking the screen and feeling relief wash through him when he saw it was from Sheila. But no text message, just an attachment, which he had to click on to see and which took an age to load. When it did appear it was as if a bucket of cold water had been poured over him. A video. A close-up of her face, one eye defiant and wary, the other bruised, half-closed with a cut above it, her mouth taped with what looked like duct tape, her cheeks streaked with mascara. Then the phone pulled away from her face to reveal that she was on a toilet seat, her arms behind her, dressed in a short skirt he'd never seen her in before and her tights crumpled at her thighs. He felt sick. From what he could see of the fittings and the black and white tiled wall behind her, it was not a bathroom he recognized. The video was all of ten seconds long.

His immediate response was to dial back her number, but the phone was switched off. The initial relief upon seeing her number had been replaced by fear and anger. He stood up, hands clenched. His phone rang; this time the number was withheld, meaning it could only be one person. He pressed the green talk button on the screen.

'You fucking bastard,' he shouted.

'Ah, Julian, I thought that would grab your attention, old comrade. Sorry I sent it from her phone but I don't have a camera on mine. I'm old fashioned that way.'

'I'll break your neck if you hurt her.'

'My dear fellow, as you have seen from the video, I have already hurt her. But that is nothing compared to what can happen to her. She is an English rose, Julian, and there is something about her, something I find quite appealing. She likes to share her feelings—'

'Listen, you sick bastard—'

'No. You listen. I have asked you to do something for me. I need you to do it before the end of the night. I want you to focus your mind on it and when you get tired, I want you to look at the video again so you are, what do you say, rejuvenated. I will send you another video in, let's say, eight hours, and this time she won't look as attractive as she does now.' The phone went dead and Julian flung it against the back of the sofa, then immediately retrieved it and checked it was OK. He'd let Boris get to him. He should have played it cool. But when he looked at the video again, and again, the anger welled and he threw his glass at the wall where it shattered into tiny imperfect cubes that skittered noisily across the wooden floor, the amber whisky flowing down the wall blurring through his indignant tears. Boris held what was dearest to him – he had no choice but to deliver.

He wiped his eyes, pulling himself together. He wasn't the one beaten and tied up. He looked at his stupid triangle of fears again, crossed out *being unattached*, which now looked crass, and wrote instead *being without Sheila*.

THIRTY-NINE

Mojgan was lying on the hotel bed, her back supported by numerous pillows, her freshly washed hair spread out to dry, netbook on her lap, analysing the information downloaded from the key-logger taken from Rami's computer. Every keystroke had been recorded. Every website and password with it. A whole day's worth. She enjoyed this bit of the process, she had to admit, even though it could also be depressing. She called it 'peeling the onion', where someone's life unfolded before her in thin layers of websites visited, medical conditions searched for, emails sent, videos watched. From the sort of pornography viewed (she had seen it all, some of it harmless, but sometimes she had to physically block the screen with her hand before its unpleasantness was imprinted on her brain) to the shopping sites visited, to the news sites and blogs read, to the balance in their bank accounts. She could build up a detailed picture of someone that was often in stark contrast to the image of respectability and self-assurance they tried to present in public.

Rami Haddad was a Lebanese Maronite Christian whose parents had been killed by Palestinians in Lebanon. This she knew because of certain emails he'd replied to from someone in the USA who'd contacted him thinking he might be related to the Haddads from a village in north Lebanon. He was also, based on an online credit card transaction, a paid-up member of a casino in London, and gambled online during work hours using real money. He had visited, among work-related sites, something called Ruby's Secrets, which turned out to be an agency where the women charged from £300 to £500 an hour and £750 to £2,000 a night. Curious about what they had to do for that sort of money, a perusal of the website explained that they were 'companions' who could accompany you to dinner or the theatre, and that many were 'graduates from top universities', although the pictures of them, once she logged in using Rami's password, showed them in various poses designed to be 'sexy', in expensive-looking underwear, and each had a small biography of their interests (contemporary fiction, cinema, current affairs, etc.), their vital statistics, including whether they were 'natural' – which Mojgan took as a reference to breasts – and a list of the services they offered, most of which were acronyms that Mojgan couldn't decipher. Some things were spelled out more clearly – things that wouldn't even have occurred to Mojgan to do. She made no judgement about these women; they had prostitutes in Iran (the Head of Vice in Tehran had been caught in a brothel with five of them a few years ago), although online agencies such as this were non-existent, as far as she knew, and she ought to know.

Out of curiosity she checked the page Rami had looked at. The woman on it looked familiar. Yes, of course; it was difficult to tell because she was posing in underwear and her face was not completely visible but it was definitely her – the woman she had passed in the lobby at Hadfish when she'd left. Beside her 'services offered' it said, like some of the others, GFE. She was about to look it up when her mobile phone vibrated twice on the bed beside her. She picked it up to see a text message from the usual 'Number Unknown'.

Call us now.

She felt a lurch in her chest. She had never had a message like that, couched in such direct terms. Call *us* now? Farsheed would have used the agreed code if he'd needed to speak to her; this wasn't from him. She would have to recall the number in Tehran, the line to the office. It was four p.m. here which meant it was eight o'clock there. With trembling fingers she replaced the SIM card in the phone, switched it on and dialled the number. There was a delay before it rang with an other-worldly distant sound. It rang. After twenty-odd rings it was answered.

'Yes?' said a female voice.

'It's Bahamin. I'd like to speak to my uncle.'

'OK. Let me find him and I'll ask him to call you back. Does he have your number?'

'Yes, he does.' She hung up and changed the SIM card yet again, putting the next one in and cutting the old one into pieces with some nail scissors. She then waited, taking the phone into the bathroom when she needed to use the toilet, making sure she still had a signal. Perhaps she was going to be asked to abort the mission. But then why not just send the abort code, or why hadn't Farsheed contacted her through the word game? Just to be sure, she logged in as *Mawlana* and left a message for *Shamsuddin*, who'd had no activity since their last game twenty-five hours ago. It had been hours since she'd eaten, yet the gnawing in her stomach wasn't hunger, although she knew she should eat. But she didn't want to leave in case she got the call while she was out, and this wasn't the sort of hotel that did room service. She drank water instead.

To distract herself she looked further at what Rami had been up to on his computer. Among various emails he had written was one to another software company to say that he was pleased to tell them that Hadfish's head of development, Julian Fisher, was now dedicating his whole time to working on their contract and would definitely have something to them 'by the end of tomorrow'. The email mentioned that, 'as agreed', he would update someone called Boris, 'should there be a problem'.

The call came as she was dozing on the bed, half watching TV: a talent show similar to the one in Farsi she and Farsheed watched back home made by exiled Iranians and broadcast from London where they picked it up, like millions of other Iranians, via their illegal satellite dish on the roof. She muted the TV and answered the call.

'Hello?'

'Bahamin?' She recognized the stern voice of Farsheed's boss.

'Yes, Uncle.'

'You need to go home, Bahamin.'

'But Uncle, I haven't finished my studies.'

'You will finish your studies at home.'

Was he calling from Baku? She wanted to ask if she could talk to Farsheed.

'My cousin, the one with the glasses, he is still with you?' A long pause at the other end. 'Uncle?'

'Your cousin has been in an accident. You must go home to visit.' She felt herself go dizzy even though she was sitting on the bed. On TV a boy with a Justin Bieber haircut was silently singing, beseeching the audience. 'Bahamin?'

'Is he OK? What kind of accident?' she asked.

'My dear, it is not the time to—'

'Just tell me, Uncle. Do not spare me.'

'It was a car accident. A work-related car accident. Return home as soon as possible. It is not safe.' He hung up before she could quiz him and, out of habit, she removed the SIM card and cut it repeatedly with her scissors until it was in unnecessarily tiny pieces, adding them to the others on the bedside table. She didn't like the fact that he had hung up; it gave her a bad feeling. There would be little point in ringing back – she would just get the duty officer again and no one would return her call.

Instead she got on the Internet, scouring newsfeeds for news from Baku, looking at more and more obscure news sites until lighting upon a short item on a local Baku newspaper website in Azeri about a car crash just outside Baku in which three Iranian tourists had been killed. No other cars were involved in the accident. No suspicion of foul play was mentioned. *A work-related car accident.*

The gnawing in her gut, the crushing feeling in her chest, the silent scream from a primal part of her brain: all these things told her that, without any doubt, her beloved Farsheed was in that car.

FORTY

Boris couldn't understand why they couldn't get it right. He got the impression, from her accent, that the woman on the other end was Polish.

'I booked her before, the English girl.' It had been difficult to find an English girl he'd liked in the plethora of escorts that worked in London. They were mostly eastern European or Russian, and he really wanted that repressed sexuality (or at least an ersatz version of it) that middle-class English women exuded like no other. It was a perfume; he could smell it. That's why he'd had to go upmarket, paying over the odds for someone with the education to be able to talk about books and philosophy before stripping to reveal very expensive underwear. Talking to Sheila, being enclosed with her in the small room, drinking wine, had reminded him of his suppressed needs. As he got older he needed to find his pleasures where he could, even if it meant paying for them. Also, there was a certain frisson to be had with having a woman come to the house while Sheila was imprisoned upstairs. And who knew when he would get another chance? He could feel things were closing in on him; he could see a long future without women.

After some dithering the Polish woman at the other end told him that he would be contacted within the hour. They never gave out personal contact details, and when he got the call it would show up as a withheld number, a small detail that reminded Boris that no matter how friendly and intimate the woman sounded on the phone, he was still living a fantasy that he paid for. But then most of his life had been about sustaining fantasies of one form or another – ones that were far larger and involved a lot more people than just himself and a woman pretending to find him fascinating. Fantasies masquerading as belief systems and not recognized as such.

While he waited for the phone call he opened his journal and tried to find something in it that would provide some solace. He found his page with the three headings, the three walls of his prison, as he saw them. He needed reassurance, something to tell him that what he was doing was right. He flipped through the earlier entries, the cuttings, the quotes, the numbers: plenty there to justify his actions, but would his actions have any effect? There was an inevitability about the path that his countrymen were going down, about where it led, so their actions were easy enough to predict. It was like watching the unfolding of a Greek tragedy, when you knew everything was going to end badly and all you could do was watch the flawed characters destroy themselves and everyone around them. All he was hoping was to lessen the destruction that was dealt in the process, reduce the collateral damage, as it was called. One of his phones rang and he still couldn't tell from the ring which one it was, satellite or mobile. It was the mobile, a withheld number. He spoke to her, her voice softening his mind a little, her promise to come round as soon as she could hardening his cock a little.

FORTY-ONE

J ulian was taken aback when he opened the door. Half hoping to see Sheila, despite the fact that she had a key and wouldn't have needed to ring the doorbell, he was instead faced with the diminutive figure of Salma, her eyes reddened and puffy, her head and neck wrapped in a black headscarf, the edges overhanging her face like a hoodie, leaving only her small oval face visible. She was holding on to the handle of a wheeled suitcase with one hand and in the other held a small gun pointed at his midriff. She stepped forward, signalling to Julian that her intention was to enter the house. She closed the door behind them and gestured with the gun.

'What do you want?' he managed to say.

'I need access to the control unit you have been working on,' she said. Her voice was hoarse.

'Who are you?'

'Please, where is it?' she asked, pointing the gun in his general direction.

'It's in the other room.' He led her into the living room and pointed to the circuit board connected to his laptop.

'Go and sit down,' she said, pointing at the sofa with her gun.

'Are you working with Boris?' he asked, going docilely to the sofa and sinking into the cushions. He felt oddly detached from what was happening, as if watching the whole thing through a dirty window.

'I don't know this Boris,' she said. She pulled a netbook from the outer pocket of her suitcase. 'It is OK to unplug it?' she asked.

'Yes, I'm done.'

She unplugged the board from his laptop and reconnected it to her netbook. 'I need you to explain what you have done,' she said. She had put the gun down next to her netbook on the coffee table and the question was matter-of-fact rather than threatening, as if they were collaborating programmers. The gun was on the wrong side of the netbook from Julian's tentative jumping-up-to-grab-it thought which he abandoned as soon as he had it, for no other reason than he no longer cared what she did to the circuit board. As long as she didn't take it away, which didn't look like her intention, then he was happy. 'How have you managed something that doesn't alter the code?' she asked. 'Surely they'll check for any changes that you haven't documented.'

Julian smiled, actually pleased that here was someone who could appreciate what he had done.

'Yes, they'll check the code of the actual control unit, but they won't check everything on the chip.'

She frowned and her fingers worked quickly over the keyboard. The professional in Julian wanted to go round and see what she was doing but he thought it best to stay put.

'What software are you using to access the chip?' he asked, genuinely curious.

'Eclipse.'

'I use the same.'

The young woman looked at him as if he were stupid, which she made him feel, and he realized that her puffed eyes and reddened nose were caused by crying. Lots of crying.

'So what have you done?' she persisted.

'These chips come with their own operating system, right? A library of software: print functions, temperature monitors, boot-up routines—'

'I know what an operating system is.'

'Of course, sorry. The point is that nobody, in all my years of programming embedded software, has ever checked these things. Even on the most sensitive of projects. I mean, all that stuff is just taken for granted. All they care about is the stuff you've been paid to write, not the stuff that comes on the chip in the first place. People treat them as blank slates but they're not.' Julian swore her dark eyes lit up for a second in recognition of what he was talking about.

She went back to the keyboard and hunched over the small screen. 'So you've added a new library function,' she said, in what Julian wanted to believe was a complimentary tone.

'No, I've amended an existing function, one that monitors the temperature of the chip, so it now has a dual function. It just needs the GPS coordinates adding and those will be checked against target coordinates that are programmed into the UAV. I assume that is what you are interested in?'

Her fingers left the keyboard and she studied him. 'Who told you that? This Boris person?'

'Yes. Are you sure you don't know him?'

She ignored him, taking out her mobile phone and pressing a button on the side. A memory card popped out. She stuck it into the side of her netbook, ran her finger over the touchpad then tapped it. She waited for something to happen on her screen. Julian guessed she was loading stuff into the function he had hacked.

'Your partner knows him,' she said.

He sat up. 'Sheila knows him?'

She frowned. 'No, your partner. Your business partner.'
'Rami?'

She nodded and he was going to ask her how she knew, then remembered that she'd spent two days in Hadfish. It wouldn't have been too difficult for someone with her skills to get into Rami's email account. She'd probably got his home address from Naomi's computer.

'I'm confused about all this. So do you work for the Israelis?'

She didn't answer, instead working at her netbook, then she sat back and flexed her fingers. She would be compiling what she'd just added in order to post it to the chip. She seemed less distraught now that she'd been working for a while. Julian took his drink from the table, thinking if she was working for Israel she could have just done this back home, or in Leeds.

'This Rami uses prostitutes,' she said, apropos of nothing, her tone still matter-of-fact.

Julian laughed. 'Whoa, steady on, lady, he has a girlfriend.'

She looked at him again as if he were stupid and shook her head. 'He gambles also.'

Bloody hell, Julian thought, could that be true? Maybe that's where the expenses money had gone – gambling. Was there no one who could be relied on?

'Are you nearly finished?' he asked. 'I need to get this to the client and get Sheila back.'

'Sheila is your wife?' she asked, stressing the 'la' in Sheila's name.

'She's not my wife, she's my partner, not my business partner, but my . . . life partner, which is why I was confused earlier when you . . . Never mind, just finish, please.'

She nodded. 'I'm debugging now,' she said. 'It's important.' After some moments of odd silence she unplugged the circuit board and put away her netbook. 'Do you have a pen and paper?'

Not wanting to go anywhere, he took the Scrabble box from the shelf underneath the coffee table and recovered the score pad and a pencil. The woman's face changed when she saw the Scrabble board, like he'd shown her something inappropriately personal.

'You play this game with her?' Her voice had changed.
'Yes, we play Scrabble.'

'With Sheila, your life partner?' It sounded natural, that phrase, when she said it, as if it were a perfectly normal way to describe someone.

'Yes,' he said as she took the pencil and pad.

'I saw her at Hadfish, no?'

'Yes, that was her.'

She nodded as if this explained something. 'You have to get her back from where?'

'From Boris,' Julian said.

She closed her eyes and moved her lips, then wrote something down carefully on a fresh sheet of the score pad, ripped it off and handed it to him. It looked like an email address, nondescript, just letters and numbers, an @ sign.

'What's this for?'

'I'm hoping whoever you give it to will know what to do with it. You will give the circuit to Boris in return for your Sheila, yes?'

'Yes.'

'And he asked you to do the work on it?'

More nodding.

'Then he will know what to do with it.' With that she put her netbook away, took her case and the gun and went to the door.

'I will leave this' – holding up the gun – 'next to the front door, in case you need it. Good luck.'

As he heard the front door close he wanted to ask about how she'd got Naomi to stay at home but he already felt like he'd been subjected to a barrage of toxic information. He sat back, exhausted and disconcerted, as if he'd just woken from a vivid yet surreal dream.

FORTY-TWO

Once Salma, or whatever her real name was, had left, Julian pondered his options. He thought more alcohol might help, but then thought better of it; something told him that tonight, of all nights, he needed to regain his wits and keep hold of them. He didn't have a clue what was going on, and although he had done what Boris had asked, there was no sign of Sheila, and it wasn't as if he could call Boris – his calls were always made from a withheld number. So here he was, pacing up and down, frustrated and helpless.

On the basis that any action was better than none he decided to see what Salma had programmed into the circuit board, so he hooked it up to his laptop and looked for changes. She had modified his library function slightly and added a range of GPS coordinates, rather than specific ones. He typed a few into Google Maps, just out of curiosity, and they popped up in Iran, seemingly in the middle of nowhere. From what Boris had told him he'd expected them to be in Israel. He was about to delve a little closer into what this meant when he was brought to his feet by a lightning thought. *Fuck. Fucking idiot. Fucking GPS coordinates.* He shook his head at his own stupidity. Sheila's smartphone, since he knew it had location services switched on (he'd done it himself when she'd asked him), would have logged its position when the video was taken and the GPS coordinates would be embedded in the fucking video. He sat down again, and it took him a frustrating five minutes to find and download some software that could read embedded metadata in videos. Then he plugged in his phone and copied the video on to the laptop. The GPS coordinates were revealed like a charm. Fingers trembling with anticipation, he had to key the numbers into Google Maps three times before getting them right, and the little flag popped up on the north side of Onslow Square in Kensington. Yes, she'd mentioned a house on Onslow Square. Zooming out, he realized it was not that far away – five minutes in the car. Unable to stand still, he paced to the French doors and back to help him think.

He could call the police, but that would involve a long-winded explanation of what had happened, about the blackmail, and about why he was being blackmailed. He could lie to them, just say that she'd been kidnapped, but then things could get messy and there could be a stand-off. Furthermore, Boris probably had some connection with the Israeli security service and by default the British. He just wanted Sheila to be safe and back at home, that was his priority. Calling the police might do that, but that seemed like abrogating his responsibility to act; after all, he had caused this situation in the first place with his lies and omissions. Talking to the police would also take too long and he wasn't going to wait until morning. He could be there in minutes. It was time to put things right. He thought about ringing Rami but if Salma said he knew Boris then he would probably warn him. Julian needed to act directly, to go to the source of all his woes.

He put the circuit board in a Jiffy bag, gathered his phone and wallet and headed for the door. There in the hall, on the narrow antique table he and Sheila had picked out in Notting Hill some years ago, was the small handgun that the woman had threatened him with. She'd left it for him, as she'd said she would. If Boris was resistant to giving Sheila up, and became violent, he might need it to subdue him. He picked up the weapon and tucked it into the back of his trousers, covering it with his jacket. The cold steel felt reassuring against his coccyx, and he was glad to have it, even though he hadn't a bloody clue how it worked.

FORTY-THREE

A s soon as he drove to the end of the street he had come up with a potential problem: GPS coordinates just weren't that accurate; the exact house was going to be difficult to find. If only he'd paid more attention to what she'd said about it, or shown more interest, but there was no reason on earth she would have told him the exact address. But she might have told her assistant, David. Julian had met him once at a barbecue they'd thrown when Sheila had set up her little business, but he had no way of contacting him and didn't even know his last name. There might be a record or an address in Sheila's office at the house, or even better, an address of the house on Onslow Square. He drove round the block only to find his parking space was gone. Typical. He reversed back up the street to a space he had passed. He was about to get out of the car when he saw a young couple approach his front door. They were dressed like Jehovah's Witnesses but it was far too late for proselytizing. They pressed the doorbell. Julian, who could make them out by the light he'd left on in the hall coming through the frosted glass of his front door, didn't recognize them. He was about to get out and see who they were when the man seemed to shield the woman as she bent down to pick something up from the porch. Then she stood up and the door miraculously opened. Julian was so surprised it took him a few seconds to realize that no one had opened the door to them – she must have picked the lock. The door closed behind them. Julian thought about going into the house and challenging them with the courage imparted by the weapon tucked into his jeans, but the hall light went out and this gave him pause; these were people who were happier working in the dark. Julian felt scared, and besides, his overwhelming desire was to get to Sheila; nothing in the house was worth a confrontation. He restarted the car and resumed his journey.

Once he had parked on the north side of Onslow Square, which is where Google Maps indicated the video had been taken, Julian had no clue as to which house to go to. He spotted Boris's taxi, the bonnet of which was cold to the touch, but there was no knowing how close to the house it was parked. If anything Boris may have deliberately parked it on the opposite side of the square. It was after eleven, and Julian walked by the houses, discounting those where there were lights on behind blinds or curtains, or which had plants outside the door, or any sign of life at all. The houses were big, multi-storeyed and elegant. Sheila would make a healthy commission from it, if it ever sold. He knew little about Sheila's finances, or how much she made. She had never asked him for money, and had insisted on a joint mortgage of their house, and he paid half of the payment into her account every month. She also took every care to pay half the bills, to the point of distraction. They could afford to be relaxed about it, and Julian didn't really care – to him his money was her money, but with her it was a matter of principle. It was irksome, and whenever he'd mentioned it she'd mutter something about not wanting to end up like her mother, which, when he thought about it, implied to Julian that she thought he was like her father, who, from what he could gather, was emotionally crippled. Well, that was something he was determined not to be.

He was torn between two houses that looked unoccupied. They

were about five houses apart and he walked towards one as the ticking diesel engine of a slow-moving taxi pulled up outside it. He stopped, stepping back behind one of the white pillars that framed the entrances to the houses. He couldn't see the door from where he was but heard heels on the steps and a woman walked from the house to the taxi. Her movement looked familiar to him but the light was dim and she only appeared for a few seconds before getting into the taxi. As it passed him he looked inside and the woman looked out at him. It was Cassie, her eyes widening in recognition.

He went up the steps she'd just left and took the gun from his trousers before trying the doorbell, which didn't work. He was about to use the brass knocker instead when the door swung open to reveal Boris, his smiling face eerily lit by the sodium glow of the street light.

FORTY-FOUR

B oris looked far from surprised to see Julian standing there, and didn't lose the smile when he saw the gun Julian was brandishing in a manner mimicked from many films. No doubt Cassie had immediately rung Boris after seeing him. For his part Boris was armed with a plastic cup of a full-bodied red wine, judging by the smell coming from it.

'Come in, old comrade,' he said, stepping aside. Julian stepped inside and Boris closed the door quietly behind him, putting the chain on. 'Through there,' he gestured with his cup. Julian obeyed, following the light from a candle that burned in a back room. 'No electricity, I'm afraid.'

'Where's Sheila?' Julian asked, lifting the gun. He didn't know if the safety was on or not, but maybe Boris couldn't tell in this light. It had also bruised his coccyx on the ride over.

'She's safe,' Boris said, nodding at the gun. 'Where did you get that?'

'Never you mind,' Julian said, trying to sound menacing. Boris shrugged and took a deep drink.

'What the fuck is going on, Boris? And no flim-flam.'

'Flim-flam? What is it you want to know?' He sat down in a camping chair that was set up next to a sleeping bag on an inflatable mattress. The candle stood on a sideways box that contained Boris's large collection of books. Julian saw the leather-bound diary that he had spotted in Boris's taxi, open with a pen in the middle. Boris picked it up and closed it, carefully binding it before putting it next to a tiny chess set on the makeshift table. Julian had to wonder how Boris, with fingers like his, managed to move the pieces.

'Why don't we start with what Cassie was doing here?'

'Cassie? You mean Cassandra. She was providing a service,' Boris said, smiling.

'What do you mean? What sort of service?'

'A personal service. One that requires skill and dexterity and at my age a little imagination and perseverance. Anyway, she is not relevant to the matter in hand, like I say, that's a personal matter.'

Julian shook his head to rattle his brain into making sense of what was going on.

'But she's my business partner's girlfriend,' he said.

'She's nobody's girlfriend, Julian. She's Rami's girlfriend when I pay her to be.'

'Pay?'

'You are straying from what is important. Focus, *tovarisch*, focus.'

Julian rubbed his temples. Maybe that's what the woman in his house had meant about a prostitute. He'd had an odd feeling about Cassie, about the way fake way she'd interacted with Rami. But Boris was right, this wasn't important at the moment. 'OK then, the woman who was at Hadfish, pretending to be the office manager, she came to my house tonight,' Julian said. 'She did some work on your control board. Who is she?'

'Ah, the woman you thought I'd put there. What does she look like, this woman?'

'Middle Eastern, small, lots of black hair, sometimes she wears a headscarf, attractive.'

'Then I am sorry I don't know her.'

'I said no bullshit.'

'So this is what flim-flam means. You think you know a language . . .'

'Enough, Boris, enough. You blackmailed me to work on this thing, ostensibly to test its vulnerability in the face of GPS spoofing, presumably by the Iranians. And then this woman, the same one who somehow got herself working at Hadfish, comes into my house at gunpoint and adds GPS coordinates that are in Iran, not Israel. She told me you know Rami.'

'She knows who I am?'

'She knows of you. From Rami, or from his emails or computer.'

Boris shook his head as if disappointed, whether in her or Rami, Julian couldn't tell. 'Did she give you the gun?'

Julian nodded. 'Is she Iranian?'

'Probably,' said Boris. 'Now put the gun away and have a seat.'

But Julian focused on why he was really there. 'Where's Sheila? I've got the control unit with me. It works. I tested it and that woman tested it when she'd done her bit.' He took the small Jiffy bag from his jacket pocket. 'Here.'

Boris shook his head. 'I don't want it. You have to get it back to the company, through your partner. It's important it goes through the right channels. I'm quality control, remember, not the client.'

Exasperated, Julian put the Jiffy bag back in his jacket. 'Where's Sheila, then. Is she here?'

'Sheila is nearby. I'm sorry I had to keep her but it was imperative that you finish and she was the only thing that seemed to motivate you into action. I didn't hit her, by the way; that was an accident that I exploited. I can try to explain things, a little, anyway.'

'I don't really care enough to hear your justifications for blackmail and kidnapping.'

Boris put the cup down and looked annoyed. 'You don't care? You don't care why all this has happened? You used to care at one point, didn't you, *tovarisch*? You were prepared to betray your country, the company you worked for, your workmates, even lie to Sheila. Now you claim you don't care. Now, all you want is to have your cosy little bourgeois life back, where all you have to worry about is whether your house has lost value in a recession caused by short-term money-grabbing capitalists. I really think, don't you, that banks should have five- and ten-year plans like we used to have back in the USSR.'

Julian snorted but Boris was on a roll.

'That's the trouble with the world today – people just sit back and let things happen to them. They moan, sometimes they sign things, sometimes they give money. Whatever happened to people acting on their beliefs?'

'Because when they do, like taking to the streets to protest, it makes no difference. The days of a proletarian revolution are over, Comrade Reznik,' Julian said.

'Maybe you're right, which is why sometimes other forms of action become justified.'

'Really? You mean terrorism?'

Boris shook his head but Julian ignored it.

'This from the man who came to me talking about making himself comfortable in old age. All your ex-KGB friends are probably oligarchs now, while you're still grubbing around in the same murky intelligence field you were thirty years ago, just with different puppet-masters. And while we're at it, you were the one who came to me way back when, saying I could make a real difference in the world. Well, that didn't really happen, did it? So don't start lecturing me on what I chose to do with my life after I came to my senses. I was deeply unhappy, creeping around, lying to people.'

'You have a point, if crudely put. But this isn't about you, Julian, and it was never about money, it's about setting constraints, reining in people who've gone rogue. I just mentioned the pension because I thought money would appeal—'

'So this Iranian woman *is* working for you?'

Boris shook his head. 'No, no, no, she was working for someone else; a young man I had an understanding with. You see, I've been disappointed a lot of my life, Julian. Disappointed with the Soviets, and now disappointed with the Zionists. I thought when I moved to Israel that I'd be going home, but far from it. In Russia I was looked down on for being a Jew, even though I didn't feel like one, and in Israel I was looked down on for being a Russian, even though I tried, *am trying*, to be a proper Jew.'

'But you told me the other day, in your taxi, that you looked for Zionist Jews to help you out.'

'I told you what you needed to hear at the time, Julian, you should know how this business works by now. Listen. I've been doing a lot of reading, working through things, and it's difficult for me to move on at my age. In my profession, I have few options, but I want to have done something, however small, to stop the madness, to reclaim being a Jew.'

Julian shrugged, impatient with Boris's self-obsession and not really understanding what he was on about. 'You're part of the madness, Boris. Retire, go fishing. Play chess,' he said, pointing at the chess set.

'Yes, I could retire, but I don't want to live it out in a prison, even if I am provided with a pension.' He shrugged. 'I suppose I could join a security firm. There are hundreds of them now – even the intelligence community is being contracted out to the private sector. But that would mean just more "grubbing around" as you so accurately put it.' He picked up the plastic cup and drained it, and with some difficulty, given his bulk, level of inebriation, and the low seat of the camping chair, got up to look for the wine bottle.

'So *you* were working for the Iranians, is that it?' Julian asked as Boris emptied the bottle into the plastic cup.

'No, it was neither one thing nor the other. Are you sure you don't want some wine?'

'So why me? Why did you need me?'

'I needed your skills, obviously, but I also needed a cut-out, someone who would deliver but didn't know what he was delivering, someone over whom I had leverage. I needed a means of exchange, a go-between. Although I don't know if they've fulfilled their part of the bargain. Did she give you anything, the attractive woman?'

Julian remembered the email address she'd written down. He threw the gun on to the sleeping bag and took the Scrabble score sheet from his wallet. 'Is this what you're expecting?'

Boris took it and looked up at Julian. 'She gave you this?'

'Yes, although she didn't seem to know who it was for.'

'It's for me, old chap. It's for me. It's the other side of the equation. Criss-cross, like the film.'

Julian understood nothing except that Boris had lost his ideologically and religiously confused, vodka-addled mind.

'Where's Sheila, Boris?'

'She's in a room at the top of the stairs,' he said. 'The key is in the door.' As Julian got to the door Boris called out to him. Julian turned to see him stuffing things into a case and zipping it up. 'Here are her things. I've put everything in there.' It was the case she'd taken the night she'd left.

Boris looked terribly old in the candlelight as Julian took took the case.

'Listen,' Julian said. 'I don't know if this is important but there was a couple, a man and woman. I saw them break into my house when they thought I'd left.'

Boris's eyes flashed in the dim light. 'How long?' he asked.

'Twenty minutes ago.'

'OK, Julian, whatever happens, get that control board back to Rami as soon as you can – he'll know what to do. But tell him nothing of our conversation.' He grabbed Julian's upper arms. 'Now get Sheila and leave, *tovarisch*, as quick as your little bourgeois feet can carry you.'

FORTY-FIVE

Boris looked curiously at the small weapon, a silly little Ruger, and smiled. Julian, probably without realizing it, had had the safety on. He studied the email address given him and switched on the satellite phone. He dialled. His boss answered on the third ring.

'Where the hell have you been?' he said in Russian. 'You are out of order not calling in. What's going on?'

'Don't worry, I've got it. Do you have a pen?'

'You need to go home right away.'

'Home?'

'Yes, *tovarisch*, home.'

'Do you have a pen?'

'Have you had a breakdown or something? You should know the problems we've been having here. We've had to take action with our friends.'

Boris had to consciously relax his grip so as not to crush the phone. 'What action?'

'An accident is all it took, Borya, just a car accident. The roads here are terrible. Today's spies are not so good in the field, they spend too much time in front of a computer.' Another laugh while Boris desperately tried to process what was being said.

'This must be a scrambled line, right? Write this down. It's the email address I told you I could get. You need to give it to the cyber-spooks, they'll know what to do with it, they were briefed before I left. They should already have an appropriate video ready containing the Trojan.' He carefully read out the email address and asked his boss to repeat it.

Someone was vigorously using the brass knocker on the front door.

'I've got it. This is good, Borya, but it's not brilliant. What about the other thing you were there for?'

'The other thing is taken care of as well, that will go back via the commercial channels. Everything was a success.'

'Good. Now get yourself back home. Your local office has sent someone to help. There's a flight in the morning.'

Boris laughed at the word help. 'They're here now.'

'Good. Go with them. I'll see you back home for debriefing. Your methods, Borya, have got me in a lot of trouble. We'll need to sit down and sort it out.'

'You have the email address, you'll soon have the control unit. Use them. I have done my bit to ensure that the motherland remains secure. Now I am retiring, comrade.' Boris enjoyed the stunned silence at the other end for a few seconds before hanging up, then switched off the phone. The front-door knocker was used with more urgency. At this rate the neighbours would be alerted. He held the piece of paper Julian had given him against the candle and let it burn, then rubbed the ashes to powder; technology was such that nothing was private any more.

He was pleased at how things had come together, especially with so many variables. He regretted what had happened to Sheila, but then she may come out of it stronger than before. Julian too, for that matter. And as for whatever happened in Baku, it would be a shame if the earnest young man hadn't lived to see that Boris had kept his side of the bargain. Picking up the tiny gun, which his hand enveloped completely, he went to the bottom of the stairs and looked up. Julian and Sheila were halfway down, holding hands, uncertain as to what to do. They'd been too slow. Someone was putting something into the lock. He waved Julian and Sheila back up, gesturing that they should hide. He wiped any previous prints off the weapon with his shirt and undid the safety with his thumb, slowly drawing a round into the chamber before going to the door as it opened and was immediately restrained by the chain.

'Who is it?' he asked amiably, as if he didn't know.

FORTY-SIX

As Julian and Sheila reached the middle of the stairs someone used the door knocker and they both froze. The sound reverberated around the empty house.

'Who's that?' Sheila whispered.

Julian said nothing, thinking of the Google map of Onslow Square he'd left on the screen of his laptop which would have led them here. He looked at Sheila.

'What is it?' she asked as the knocking sounded again.

He was about to tell her about the couple who'd entered their house when Boris appeared at the bottom of the stairs, gun in hand. Whoever was at the door was trying the lock. Boris looked up and gestured urgently for them to get back. They went back into the bathroom where Julian left the door ajar so he could hear as well as get a little light from the upstairs hall window that looked on to the street since he didn't want to switch on the camping light. Sheila was pressed up against him and he reached round reassuringly.

'Who is it?' she whispered.

'A couple broke into our house just as I was coming here – they might have followed me.'

'Are they looking for you?'

'I don't know. I don't think so. They may be after Boris, or the Iranian woman, or the circuit board I was working on.' He felt for it in his pocket.

'What Iranian woman?'

Julian put his fingers to his lips as he heard Boris, with his booming voice, call, 'Who is it?' through the front door. He couldn't hear the answer but Boris opened the door and he heard voices, although it wasn't clear what was being said.

'Speak English – my Hebrew is not good enough for this level of conversation,' Boris was saying. 'Unless, of course, you can speak Russian?'

Julian wondered whether that was for his benefit but he couldn't hear the reply, just a lot of urgent talking, from both man and woman.

'Look, I've just called it in, I've spoken to the boss. Everything was a success. There's no need to panic. Let's all just calm down.'

'Is there anyone else here?' the woman asked. She must have moved to the bottom of the stairs.

'No, of course not.'

'Sure? We've just come from Julian Fisher's house.'

'Nobody is here – I spoke to him on the phone at work. The control board will go back to Leeds tomorrow, right on schedule.'

Julian fingered the Jiffy bag in his jacket again. He heard footsteps which faded and now he couldn't even hear Boris.

'Why are we hiding?' Sheila whispered. Julian didn't really have an answer. He just knew that if Boris had asked them to hide then he had good reason to. He put his fingers to his lips as he heard the voices again.

'No, I'm not going with you,' Boris was saying.

'You must come with us,' the man said. 'Those are the orders.' Then the woman must have been on the phone because she was speaking in Hebrew very fast while the man and Boris argued. Then the woman shouted for them to stop and said something he couldn't hear.

'So you've called the Cossacks,' Boris said. 'I'm not going back to Israel. I've had enough of this. *Do svidaniya.*'

The woman shouted, '*Lo,*' and a loud crack reverberated around the empty house.

Sheila clutched Julian painfully, breathing heavily in his ear. His own heart was thumping hard. He could hear the couple talking quietly, but no sound from Boris. Then it was quiet and nothing but the sound of the front door opening and closing. He heard the woman talking fast, possibly on the phone, judging by the one-sided nature of it. Then it went quiet again. Julian slipped off his shoes and opened the door with Sheila pulling at his jacket as he went on all fours to the top of the stairs. Boris was slumped against the wall, his legs splayed out on the wooden floor. It looked like he'd fallen asleep while sitting with his back against the wall were it not for the splatter of blood and brain matter higher up, where he'd been standing. He'd left a trail of it as he'd slid down the wall. The woman was kneeling by him, her back to Julian. She was removing things from his pockets, putting them into a plastic carrier bag. The trigger guard on the gun was jammed on Boris's forefinger, like a wedding ring over which a finger's grown fat, so she was having to twist it off. Her phone vibrated and she answered it, said nothing and, hanging up, went to the front door, which she opened to let in her companion. Julian froze, but he was in the dark with no light behind him. It was definitely the same couple who had been to their house. The woman put her hands to her face, shaking her head, and her companion hugged her briefly before gripping her arms and giving her a little pull-yourself-together shake.

He said something to her in Hebrew and handed her some surgical gloves which she put on. She disappeared and came back with more plastic carrier bags. The man knelt down and held Boris away from the wall as the woman put a bag over his head. Sheila touched Julian on the back and he turned to see her horri-fied face. The couple half-dragged, half-carried Boris to the front door and Julian understood that the bag on his head was to mini-mize the amount of blood and brains he left behind as they did this. They sat him up by the door – they were getting ready to take his body away. They disappeared and came back with things in bags, including Boris's books in the cardboard box. Concerned that others were on the way and that they'd search the rest of the house, Julian went back into the bathroom. He took the key from outside and locked them in the dark, but not before he saw the fear on Sheila's face. He reached out for her.

'Is he dead?' she whispered.

'Yes, he took his own life.'

'What shall we do?' she asked.

'We wait until they've gone.'

'Shouldn't we call the police?'

He took out his phone. They were lit up in a bluish light, but there was no signal. He held it up near the vent and a bar appeared then disappeared, but even if he could keep it still he would have to talk loudly and have it on speakerphone to be able to have a conversation with his arm stretched that far. He turned it off and they were plunged back into darkness. He was relieved in a way – he had no idea what he would say to the police.

'You think they'll search the house?' she asked.

'I don't see why they should,' he said, although in truth he couldn't think of a reason why they wouldn't.

'We should lock the rest of the doors up here.'

'What?'

'One locked door is odd, but if they're all locked on this floor it won't seem out of the ordinary.'

He nodded, then remembered she couldn't see him.

'The keys are in the doors,' she added.

'Won't the floors creak?' he asked.

'No, this place is solid and it's carpeted up here.'

'OK, let's do it. Take your shoes off.' He quietly unlocked the door and whispered. 'You take the back, I'll do the front. We'll meet back in here.'

'Right, but bring the keys, don't leave them in the doors.'

Julian made his way past the top of the stairs to the end of the hall and looked out of the window on to the square. A dark van pulled up outside the house and he stepped back as three men got out and came up to the house and disappeared under the porch. He heard a more gentle knocking on the door. He carefully locked his two doors, removing the keys, and met up with Sheila in the middle. They went back into the cramped cloakroom and locked themselves in. They sat on the camping mattress with their backs to the wall and waited. Indeterminate noises came from downstairs, and about forty-five minutes later someone came up the stairs and tried the door as they held their breath and each other's hand. Whoever it was moved to the other doors and tried them, went up a floor where they could hear them walking about, then went downstairs again. Julian squeezed Sheila's hand to acknowledge her idea. His eyes, growing accustomed to the dark, discerned moonlight coming through the vent high up on the outside wall. The noises from downstairs ebbed and flowed, then the front door closed and it was silent. She took her clammy hand from his.

'I don't know about you but I think we should wait until it's light,' he said. 'Just to be sure.'

'Shouldn't we call the police now?'

'And say what? What are they going to do? I suspect those people will have disappeared by the time they've finished questioning us, which could take days.'

'I was fucking kidnapped, Julian.'

'Yes, and the guy that did it has blown his brains out, isn't that enough for you?'

She blew out some air and he could picture her face. They could have put a light on but he liked it better in the dark. Their anger and frustration filled the small room like a toxic gas. He could smell her sweat and bad breath. He reached out and found her knee. 'I'm sorry,' he said.

'He said he'd known you a long time,' she said, her voice soft.

'Yes, it's a long story.'

'We've got time, why don't you tell it to me?' She found his hand.

He'd read or heard somewhere that people often had their most intimate conversations while driving or walking, as they were facing forward and were spared the inhibiting fear of the other's facial reactions to what they were saying. Or perhaps it was something to do with the distracting nature of forward movement that made self-revelation easier. He did not have the benefit of such movement but being in the dark, which removed one of the senses, seemed to help.

'I don't know where to start,' he said, surprised to find his voice wobbling.

FORTY-SEVEN

When, in due course, exhausted, their legs stiff with sitting on the floor, they ventured downstairs, trepidatious in the early light, they found the place empty. Nothing was left of Boris where his brains and hair and skull

had been plastered on to the wall, just a damp stain and the smell
of bleach remained. But Sheila noticed a small hole in the wall
above the wainscoting, at head height, perhaps where the bullet
had lodged and been removed. She would have to get it filled,
she thought, then immediately felt ashamed of thinking it. All
Boris's things had also been removed, and, Jules told her after
looking through the bay window, his taxi had gone.

'It's like last night never happened,' Jules said. It was true. It
was as if Boris had been scrubbed clean from the face of the earth.

'Let's get out of here,' she urged. He didn't argue.

They travelled the short distance home in silence and she immediately rushed upstairs, stripped and, catching just a quick glimpse
of the dark swelling around her eye, got under the shower, letting
the hot water plaster her hair to her skull and wash the last twenty-
four hours away. When she emerged, a good ten minutes later, she
could smell coffee. She was fatigued but wired, having listened to
Jules all night. He had gradually, with a little prompting at first,
unpeeled the various layers of himself. He'd revealed himself as
someone new, a stranger she didn't know existed, someone she'd
been living with. A liar, and, let's face it, a traitor, however misguided
he'd been, although to his credit he hadn't used the folly of youth
to excuse his behaviour. She examined her bruised face more
leisurely in the mirror, with the intention of disguising it as best as
she could with foundation, then decided not to put on any make-up
at all, to wear the bruise as a badge, although of what she didn't
know. Not honour exactly. A mark of respect? Reality? In a life
happily void thus far of violence it was like a rude wake-up call, a
literal slap in the face. She dressed in jeans and a white T-shirt and
went down to the kitchen, where Jules was grilling bacon and mixing
eggs with a fork. He looked her up and down and smiled, but it
was the smile of someone she didn't recognize. She poured coffee.
He scrambled eggs and flipped bacon. She checked for landline
voice messages: nothing. She plugged in her spent mobile to discover
two messages on it – one from Cassie asking whether she was OK
and one from Gulnar wondering how she was getting on with the
paperwork. She hadn't started any paperwork, but she would.

They ate in silence, the smell and taste of the food awakening
her suppressed appetite. She stole glances at him across the

counter, as if he were an attractive stranger she was on a date with and deciding whether to go home with him or not. Except she was home with him. Except he'd given her name to his KGB contact Boris so they could check up on her. Except she was mentally leafing through all the times she'd thought he was out on business when he might have been handing over military secrets. Except he was a good lover. Except he'd left his promising career at British Aerospace, citing his unwillingness to continue working to develop weapons. Except maybe that wasn't the real reason.

'God, I was hungry,' he said, pushing his plate aside and pouring himself more coffee. Then it just came out of her:

'I want you to leave,' she said, sitting up straight. He put the coffee pot down while looking at her and she couldn't bring herself to say anything more. She wanted to explain that she needed time to process all the things he had told her.

'You need time to think,' he said at last, to her relief. 'I understand. You've had a shitty twenty-four hours, and all' – he gesticulated – 'this has come as a shock.'

She wished he'd just stop talking.

He got off the kitchen stool. 'I'll shower and get some things together. I have to go to the office.'

She wanted to ask him where he would stay, what he would do. She didn't want to exhibit any concern because she might crumble had he expressed any emotion. He looked so . . . broken. She managed a nod and stopped him as he passed by, putting her hand on his forearm. 'Thanks,' she said.

He leant forward and kissed the top of her head and moved on. She was not going to cry.

FORTY-EIGHT

'I'm dissolving the partnership,' Julian said to Rami. They were sitting in the greasy spoon near Hadfish over mugs of powerful tea.

Rami was stirring sugar into his, looking into the swirling

brew. 'Why do the English have milk in their tea? I mean, where does it come from?' Rami asked.

'I think it was the Portuguese, or maybe the French,' Julian said, indulging Rami, giving him time to assimilate what he was telling him. The stirring went on longer than necessary.

'What about your guys, your coders?' Rami asked.

'They can see out the existing contracts if they want, then they'll have to find new work. It won't be difficult for them, even in this climate.'

Rami nodded. What Julian didn't tell him was that he might use the best of them in whatever venture he might set up next, but then Rami was no doubt thinking exactly the same thing.

'And Naomi?'

'I don't know yet. I'm sure between us we can find something for her.'

Rami nodded and looked over Julian's shoulder as the door opened. 'Here they come now, your lads. Maybe we should talk about something else rather than making people redundant.'

Julian looked round to see Nizar come in with two of his non-Hadfish mates, ones he'd seen in here before. Nizar nodded at him, ignoring Rami, he noticed, and they went over to the table furthest away from theirs. Julian turned back to Rami. 'You understand why I'm doing this, don't you?'

Rami grinned unpleasantly, for no reason Julian could decipher. He leaned forward and spoke in a hush. 'Because of Sheila, I presume? Isn't that why we're here?'

'Sheila?'

'Yes. I assume you've had a heart-to-heart.'

'Well, yes, but—'

'And she told you the truth. And now you feel the need to punish me.'

He wasn't sure what Rami was talking about. Did he know about Sheila's kidnapping? Cassie had been at the Onslow Square house – had she known Sheila was a prisoner there and told Rami? Had they been complicit in arranging it? He shook that thought from his head.

'It's not a matter of punishment, Rami, it's a matter of trust. You lied to me about this fucking drone job. You kept Boris informed of my progress behind my back.' He wanted to mention

the missing money but he really didn't have proof of that. Some
emotion Julian couldn't recognize distorted Rami's face for a
second.

'So it's not because I slept with Sheila, then?'

Julian felt his face burn and his hearing muffle, then gradually
it returned and he could hear the clicking of laptops from the
other side of the café, the hissing of the coffee machine behind
the counter, a lorry going by outside. Rami's face reappeared,
his eyes looking for the hurt in Julian's face. Julian tried to make
connections between what he'd just heard and what Sheila'd
said, where she'd been, when. When is what he wanted to ask
Rami, but he wouldn't give him the satisfaction that Rami was
seeking, his expectancy obvious as he waited for Julian to
demand details. Julian was determined not to ask for details. He
didn't want details.

'No, that's nothing to do with it. I didn't know about that,' he
managed to say. Rami's shoulders fell. He looked down at his tea.

'It was just the once, a couple of years ago,' he said, flattened.

Julian forced himself to say nothing, knowing Rami would fill
the silence himself.

Rami looked up and to Julian's surprise his eyes had welled
up. 'I loved her, you see. I still do.' His voice was cracking.
'But what you two had, have got, it just seems beyond my
bloody capability. Do you understand? I think I just wanted a
taste of it.'

Julian wanted to tell him that not everything was rosy in the
garden of Julian and Sheila but he was happy not to disabuse Rami
of his impression – he needed to feel superior at this point. Rami's
real intention may well have been to destroy what he couldn't have,
but then why wait until now to tell him? And this extraordinary
business of pretending Cassie was his girlfriend – it didn't seem
possible that he didn't even know that she was an escort. He wanted
to ask him, to use it as a way of getting the upper hand, but tears
were slowly running down Rami's cheeks. Most likely he and Sheila
were the result of a drunken night that had no real meaning to either
of them and Rami was indulging in the post-event rationalization
that intelligent people excel at when they don't want to admit to
being driven by their more primal urges. Julian passed him a napkin.

'Not in front of the staff, Rami.'

Rami attempted a smile and dabbed at his face. 'Look,' he said, 'I'm sorry I told you.'

Julian laughed despite himself. 'Sorry that you told me, not that it happened.'

'I mean I don't want it to become an issue between you two. She regretted it straight away, I could see that, even though she's too nice to say so. It was completely my doing, really. I seduced her, wore her down. You know what I'm like.'

'You didn't force her, presumably?'

'Well, of course not, it—'

'I think you're claiming too much credit, despite your "seduction" tecniques. It's not completely your doing, is it?' Julian, oddly mindful of his own self-control and calm – which seemed to have settled on him since unburdening himself that night in Onslow Square – drew on it to make himself even calmer. 'I'm sure she had good reason to respond to you.' It occurred to Julian that Rami was perhaps trying to make him feel better by telling him it was all his doing, but Sheila was not a passive participant in anything. The point was he didn't really care. It didn't matter any more. Time to change the subject.

'The circuit board, the UAV control unit, are they happy with it?' Julian had dropped it off at Hadfish the morning he'd left home. He'd since taken a few days off and found somewhere to stay. Naomi had been at the office and tried to speak to him, but he'd avoided her.

'Yes,' Rami said, 'they were quite impressed with your risk assessment. It went back to Israel. I've submitted a hefty invoice given . . . everything that happened.'

'Good. I'd like to see the paperwork if you don't mind, given the circumstances.'

Rami looked up. 'We could capitalize on this, Julian. The work that comes through as a result—'

'You don't give up, do you?'

He smiled, shaking his head.

'Since we're no longer touting for new business,' Julian said, matter-of-factly, 'there's not much point in you coming in to the office any more. Just email me a list of the outstanding contracts and deliverables. Once all the jobs are completed we'll formalize the dissolution of the partnership.'

Rami looked like he was going to cry again but then stood up. 'OK. I'll sort it out today. You can reach me at home if there are any issues.' Rami stuck out his hand and Julian, seeing no reason not to, took it.

Once Rami had gone, Julian sat and drank his now cold tea. He was wondering whether what he had just learnt put things between him and Sheila on a more equal footing, or whether it was a form of poetic justice inflicted on him. A karmic reckoning: one night's infidelity for years of lying. He'd come off lightly in that case. Someone was standing beside him, clearing his throat: Nizar.

'Sorry, I can see you're deep in thought. Is everything all right?'

Julian nodded.

Nizar pointed to Rami's empty chair. 'May I?'

'If this is a work thing, do you mind if we pick it up at the office? I'll be in later.'

'It has nothing to do with Hadfish,' Nizar said. Julian forced a polite smile and pushed the chair out with his foot. Nizar sat down and moved Rami's crockery to one side before placing his elbows on the table. 'You remember you asked me what we were doing in here?'

Julian nodded.

'You remember how I said we were trying to make the world a better place?'

'Yes. I assumed you were working on a game or something.'

Nizar smiled, shook his head and pushed his hair from his face. 'No, we're trying to do something much more serious and we need your help.'

FORTY-NINE

At Hadfish, Naomi, looking more miserable than he'd ever seen her, came in to his office with an envelope, closing the door behind her. She stood before his desk like an errant schoolgirl who'd been summoned by the headmaster and was waiting to hear a lecture. Julian didn't oblige, wanting her to speak first, but she just placed the envelope on his desk and folded her hands before her as if in prayer. The envelope had his name written on the front.

'What's this?' he asked, guessing it was her resignation letter.

'Money.'

'Money?'

'Three thousand pounds.'

Not understanding, he looked at her expectantly.

'It's the money that woman paid me to take my place here.'

'You took money from her.'

'I was in debt.'

'Fucking hell, Naomi,' he said, pushing himself out of his chair. It was the first time he'd sworn in front of her. 'Why are you giving it to me?'

She shifted on her feet a bit, her fingers trying to work some unseen stuff off her hands. 'I'm the one who took the money from the expense account. The London withdrawals, anyway. I saw that Rami had taken some out in Leeds and when he gave his card to me to top up the petty cash for the office . . .'

'You were that desperate?'

'I've racked up credit card bills,' she said quickly.

He looked out of the window, realizing what she'd actually done. He turned to her. 'The worst thing is that you tried to pin it on Rami.'

'I know. I'm really, really sorry, Julian. I know I've been . . . horribly deceitful. I'm not excusing what I did. That money should cover most of what I took using his card. I used some of it to pay for the hotel, I didn't feel that . . . It was like a godsend, that woman coming and offering me money. It seemed like the perfect way to repay it without anyone knowing.'

'And what about the clinical depression – was that another deceit?'

She tightened her lips and looked at the desk. He thought about them in that hotel room, them lying on the bed, her in the crook of his arm, her hand on his chest, and felt shame that he'd tried to be a comfort to her. He couldn't look at her so turned to look out at the arched roof of King's Cross in the distance.

'Are you going to call the police?' he heard her say, struggling to keep her voice level.

It hadn't occurred to him. 'No,' he said to the window, 'you've returned the money. But you should look for another job as soon as possible. We're winding Hadfish down. Ask Rami to do you a reference – you might have to email him as he won't be in the office. And for God's sake don't mention this to him.'

He heard the buzz of the office rise and recede as she opened and closed his door. He turned to look out at the coders. He'd been seeing them one by one to explain the situation, telling them the recession had hit them hard. Nizar was intent on his screen. His proposal had sounded very interesting, full of potential. Very interesting indeed.

FIFTY

Three weeks had been a long time for Julian to reflect on what had happened to him and long enough, he believed, for Sheila to come to terms with it. He'd naively thought that when Sheila had asked him to leave in order to give herself time to think, she'd need three or four days max, so he'd gone to stay in a hotel nearby. Then, when it became apparent that she'd need longer, he'd rented a furnished studio flat, which, given the prices in their area, had meant moving south of the river, to Clapham. He gave her space, but it had slowly dawned on him that this was not how he'd envisaged his coming out as a former spy would be received. Yes, there'd be initial shock, but eventually, surely, a new blossoming of their relationship would begin. She would come to see how being free of his past had made him a more pleasant person to be around. But, since deciding it best not to push her and waiting for her to ask him to come home, which she hadn't yet done, he realized that he was letting her slip away from him and that the longer they were apart the more normal it would become. So he decided to go round to the house to give her a firm ultimatum, to say, yes, he'd kept things from her, but it didn't really change who he was, and that her knowing about it should be a good thing, assuming, of course, that she was happy with the new Julian, Julian the traitor and spy.

The truth was that he hadn't really thought through what he was going to say when he rang the door bell (using the key unannounced was probably a step too far); he just knew that he had to see her, to let her see him before he became a distant memory. He'd given her twenty minutes' notice, telling her he was on his way to pick up some things, and at first she'd been reluctant, saying she was busy with something, but then relented and became quite keen that he did come round.

'I've got something to give you anyway,' she'd said.

A woman, with a foreign look to her, answered the door and for a horrible moment he thought she was a compatriot of Salma and that things weren't resolved. But she took his hand in a firm handshake and introduced herself as Gulnar. She seemed to know who he was and explained that Sheila was on the phone in the office. All these papers strewn over the dining-room table, Gulnar told him, related to the charity they'd set up. The room had essentially been turned into a launch centre for Standing Together, and this was what had kept Sheila from him. Indeed, she had kept this from him. He'd imagined, rather stupidly he now realized, that she would be sitting around moping about him, reflecting on his absence, when in fact she'd been incredibly busy and, according to Gulnar, 'done six weeks' work in just three'.

When Sheila appeared she was in one of his favourite summer dresses of hers, a sartorial contrast to Gulnar's jeans and checked shirt, and instead of the half-formed heart-to-heart he'd planned to have, he ended up revamping their website, which they'd tried to do themselves but had gone about the wrong way. Gulnar eventually left, and Julian stood in the hall, not really wanting to leave, with Sheila standing in the kitchen doorframe, her arms behind behind her, an enigmatic smile on her face.

'You've lost weight,' she said, giving him an appraising look, a slight, almost mocking smile on her face. She shifted her body under the dress and reminded him why he liked it. He was getting familiar vibes telling him to go over and remove it, just like old times. But he could have been misreading the signals, which

were highly attuned to any perception of the promise of sex (he'd
been thinking of her in that way a lot), and worried about the
consequences of doing the wrong thing. She moved from the
door and the moment passed.

'I've started running,' he said lamely.

She nodded her approval. 'You said you had to pick some
stuff up?'

'Erm, yes, but I can't remember what it was now. Didn't you
say you had something to give me?'

'Maybe it was some of this.' She pulled the thin straps off her
shoulders and shrugged her dress to the ground before stepping out
of it and walking upstairs, while he remained rooted to the spot,
watching her ascend to the top of the landing, where she turned.

'Are you coming or what?'

The next morning, drowsy and content, he asked her about
Gulnar.

'She's great; she's opened my eyes to a few things.'

'Is she a lesbian?'

She laughed. 'That's not what I meant. Trust you to focus on
that. Do you think we've done it, me and her?' she teased,
climbing on top of him. 'Maybe you'd like her to join us.' Five
frenzied minutes later they lay on their bed, nuzzling and basking.
He ran his finger over a familiar scar on her neck, the result of
a childhood accident. It was small enough that you couldn't see
it if you didn't know it was there.

'I miss this,' he said, stroking her damp belly. 'I don't just
mean the sex, I mean you, your physical presence, our bed. You
make me laugh.'

'I didn't realize how much I've missed the sex,' she said,
turning to rest her head on his chest. 'And I suppose I've been
keeping myself busy so as not to miss you. I've been determined
to be angry with you but actually it's hard work being angry all
the time.' She moved off his chest and propped herself up on
her elbow, pulling the sheet over her chest. 'I've kept something
from you, too.' Here it comes, he thought. This is it, the confession he'd wanted her to make but didn't want to hear.

'You mean other than this big charity you've formed, and your
imminent visit to Afghanistan?'

She lay on her back to look at the ceiling, and again they were facing forward, like they had been in the bathroom all night, to release their confidences. Except this time he wanted to see her.

'You know I've been sleeping in the spare room; I can't sleep in this bed on my own,' she said.

'I could come home.' When she didn't respond, he added, 'If you want.'

'There's something else we need to talk about before we—'

'I've spoken to Rami,' he said, 'if that's what it is.'

Her body hardened beside him. 'He told you?'

'Yes. He thought it was why I was dissolving the partnership; he didn't really understand why else I would want to.'

'But you haven't said anything to me.'

'I haven't really had a chance,' he said. 'Plus I felt it was up to you, really, to tell me. I wanted it to come from you, not for me to confront you with it. Do you understand?'

'Yes, of course I understand. Jules, it was just—'

'No, listen. I really don't want to know the details, believe it or not. It doesn't matter to me any more. I can sort of understand why it happened.'

She turned to him and put her head back on his shoulder. He had thought about the where and when, but hadn't dwelled on it. Better to think of it in the abstract than have details. It's the details that would hurt.

'I'm sorry, but I want you to know it didn't happen here, in the house,' she said, softly. He stroked her hair and felt her relax. 'And I feel a bit stupid about the whole sordid detective thing, with Naomi.'

'Yes, where the hell did that come from?'

'It was Cassie, she arranged it for me. We got drunk over lunch and she somehow convinced me you were seeing someone else. In fact, she organized the whole thing for me.'

'So we're square on the whole Naomi thing, right?'

She moved her head up and down on his chest.

'Speaking of the pneumatically enhanced Cassie, there's something I haven't told you about her.'

She lifted her head. 'What is it?'

'It's something so shocking that my own secret will look pathetic in comparison.'

She sat up and leaned on his chest, her hair tickling his face. 'Tell me, you bastard.'

Over breakfast, when Sheila had recovered from the excitement of learning about Cassie, claiming to have suspected it all along, then shrieking, 'Oh my god, I shared a bed with her!', and Julian was thinking about how to propose moving back home, she slapped her forehead.

'I nearly forgot – I have got something I've been meaning to give you,' she said, dashing upstairs. She came down carrying a leather journal, the one he'd seen in Boris's taxi and the house in Onslow Square.

'What the fuck?'

'It was in my overnight case, you know, the one I took . . . the one I had at the Onslow Square house. He must have put the journal in there.'

Julian recalled Boris stuffing things into her case before handing it to him.

'I haven't opened it. I'm assuming he must have put it in there for you.'

FIFTY-ONE

She didn't want to mislead Jules. She wasn't the sort to play games, or one of those women who liked to 'manage' their spouses. She did not want to change him, nor did he, she believed, want to change her, or 'improve' her, or point out her faults, of which she knew there were many. They were just not that kind of couple. She had mooted this idea that they live apart permanently, but nearby, and in theory it did appeal to her. But waking up without him, excluding the days when he stayed over before going back to his studio flat, left her disconcerted, out of sorts.

Julian was familiar. He was woven into the fabric of her life. He was great to be around and affectionate, physical. He touched her and held her hand. He made her laugh, which, she'd come to realize, was very important in a world that seemed only to get darker by the day. Yes, he could be broody, but that seemed to have eased somewhat. And there were other traits of his that she wasn't crazy about, like his dismissiveness and cynicism, but at least now she had an understanding of where they came from. But given his reaction to what she was doing with Gulnar, even that seemed to have lessened, or at least he was keeping it to himself. Another positive was that the panic attacks and mysterious ailments that had dogged Julian over the years had also abated. He had taken up running and was on some weird carb-free diet, of which the benefits were increasingly visible, especially during sex, when she secretly watched him in the mirror opposite the bed. His gut had receded, and the muscles in his arms and legs were now visible. Since that night when he'd first come round – he really should have pushed to see her earlier – they'd been enjoying more time in bed than ever before. She was getting hot and bothered just thinking about it.

She should be concentrating on what she was doing, namely preparing for her trip to Kabul and beyond. The Foreign Office website advised against all but essential travel to Kabul and advised against going anywhere else in the country. Her visa had come through without a problem, her ticket was booked and she travelled in three days' time. She was excited and apprehensive at the same time. But her senses, she noticed, were enhanced. She'd developed an interest in things that had simply occupied her periphery before, things brought briefly into focus before disappearing. But these things were important, they deserved a greater scrutiny, if only for the self-serving reason that what happened out in the world had consequences back here. She had come to understand that.

As for what Julian had done for the Russians, it was illegal, of course, or had been. But was it wrong? Misguided, yes. In her mind, if he'd been a communist then he should have been a communist openly, but he seemed to have been motivated more by a desire to curb any military and technological advantage the West might have had over the Soviets than an ideological stance against capitalism or pro-communism. He'd genuinely thought he could make a difference, but had become disillusioned, unsure of who he was, where he belonged. She suspected that, like her, he'd wanted to tread a different path from the one most people trod, one she had trodden herself for many years before understanding that something was missing.

Although she'd been angry with him for not confiding in her, not to mention disappointed and shocked, he'd actually become more attractive to her after his revelation, although obviously she hadn't told him this. Nor had she told him the full consequences of what had happened with Rami; she considered that her secret punishment. He didn't need to know, any more than she needed to know what had really gone on between him and Naomi in that hotel room for an hour. None of this mattered in the broad scheme of their relationship; they were just bumps in the road.

Jules was no longer the boring guy who developed gaming software, or whatever it was, whose existence was measured by the number of contracts his company won. All she could do now was smile when she thought that her Julian used to be a bloody spy.

She was glad that he would be back in the house when she returned from her travels. It would be something to look forward to.

FIFTY-TWO

At first, Julian couldn't make sense of Boris's leather-bound diary. It was written in a mixture of Russian, Hebrew and English. It contained glued-in newspaper clippings, mainly articles from newspapers, some in English, some in Hebrew. The handwritten English entries (written in a variety of pens and pencil) were quotes from books, mostly political in nature, dealing with Judaism and Zionism. There were also bibliographical references to books that must have been the ones he was carting around in his taxi.

After a run he showered and poured himself a beer and sat down with the journal, his bare feet resting on the badly constructed flatpack coffee table in his studio apartment. Not being able to read Russian or Hebrew, and unlikely to be able to go to anyone who could, he concentrated on the English entries, starting from the beginning. An hour in and on his second beer, Julian thought he had a picture of Boris's state of mind leading up to his suicide.

The newspaper clippings he was able to read, mostly from an English-language Israeli daily, were stories ranging from the detention of Palestinian children for stone throwing, to human rights reports of Jewish settlers on the West Bank carrying out so-called 'price-tag' attacks on Palestinian villages, to decrees from rabbis against mingling with Arabs, to demonstrations against African immigrants. These were all surpassed in number by the clippings on Iran, with reference to ex-Mossad or CIA officials declaring that no credible nuclear threat existed from Iran. There were several pages of handwritten notes referring to the International Atomic Energy Agency and the Nuclear Proliferation Treaty. Under the latter he had written:

Iran signatory, Israel not. Iran issued fatwa against owning nuclear weapons. Iran made serious offer in 2005. Iran is only NPT signatory not allowed to develop nuclear energy. Iranian nuclear weapon development = dangerous delusion to serve what purpose?

One well-thumbed page attracted his attention, titled 'Three Walls', the page divided into three sections:

a) Shoah
One long Shoah. Ongoing. 'Never again'. Sacred. Dwarfs all else. Post-traumatic stress syndrome [Trauma needs to be dealt with otherwise → Just 2% of youth feel committed to democratic principles after studying Shoah]. Fear → Defensiveness → militarisation (Hitlers are everywhere.) → Aggressiveness → Iran.
b) Israel
Nakba = catastrophe, mythologizing (e.g. making the desert 'bloom'), destroyed villages, ethnic cleansing – Ajjur, Baysamun, Beit Dajan, Danna, Iqrit, Lubya, Zarnuqa, etc. Everything justified by a) is OK.

c) Election
People either have Jewish souls or they don't.
Jewishness is a state of being, a level of consciousness, not
something you are born into. Oppression negates Judaism.
Zionism is the flip side of Judaism. Chosenness is not
imposed, it means choosing to act in a positive way.

When, tired from reading, he closed the diary, Julian discovered
a small strip of tissue paper on the table. He picked it up, knowing
instantly what it was. Boris had placed it in the diary; a way of
knowing whether it had been opened without his knowledge.
He'd taught Julian the same trick for using on his front door, or
his desk at work; trapping something small enough to be un-
noticeable between the door and frame to see if anyone had
opened it. But then Boris had obviously wanted him to see this,
although for what purpose wasn't clear. Was it to explain what
he had been up to? He was none the wiser. Had Boris been
working for Iran? It seemed inconceivable but then Julian was
no longer surprised by anything. The email address he'd given
Boris from the Iranian woman? What was that for? The 'criss-
cross' business he'd mentioned.

It was past midnight when he got into his sagging bed. He
was relieved to be moving back in to the house when Sheila
was in Afghanistan; she'd said that she wanted him to be there
when she got back, but she was happy with the current arrangement until then. Afghanistan was her milestone for moving
forward, it seemed. He was OK with that. No arguments, no
sulking, and most importantly, no bloody panic attacks. In fact,
he'd cancelled his appointment with Dr Truby, told her the
triangle thing had worked and that she shouldn't be so free and
easy with it if she still wanted two holidays abroad every year.
He too had decided to apply himself to something different: the
project Nizar had asked him to get involved in. A further meeting
with him had fleshed out some of the bones and sparked some
ideas of his own.

But his thoughts, as he turned off the light, were of Boris.
He couldn't sleep, and it wasn't just the lack of support in the
mattress; something niggled him. Then, just as he was drifting
off, it yanked him back into consciousness. He sat up and

switched on the light. This was the thing: Boris hadn't wanted Julian to have the journal, he just hadn't wanted it to fall into the hands of his masters, for them to understand the real state of his mind, his disillusionment and what that might mean. He'd wanted the drone control board to go back to Israel and to be placed in the drones without any suspicion to fall on it at all. The email address he had passed on from the enigmatic woman from Iran had been a form of *quid pro quo*.

He wondered, as he turned off the light and settled back down, what had become of her.

FIFTY-THREE

When Mojgan arrived back in Tehran via Germany and Turkey, nobody met her, so she went straight to their apartment. Except now it was her apartment. Before even unlocking the door she knocked on her neighbour's door across the hall to give her the Herceptin she'd acquired. She had to put up with a couple of minutes of gushing, tearful gratitude before being able to establish that nobody had come to Mojgan's apartment, no unknown visitors had rung her doorbell or asked about her.

Once in her own place she crashed, spending thirteen hours asleep before waking to find his things everywhere, sensing his absence, smelling the sweat in his shirt in the laundry basket, crying and ignoring the ringing phone. On the third day her neighbour knocked on her door, concerned for her, or maybe just nosy. She stood in the hall with a plate of rice and lamb. Mojgan took the food, so as not to appear ungrateful, and closed the door. She picked at the rice, threw the rest away, and after a decent interval placed the washed plate outside the neighbour's front door.

On the fourth day she picked up the ringing phone, because at some point she had to, and someone from the ministry that she didn't know asked her to come to an address not far from where she lived. They told her to be there at nine the following morning. It was the precise nature of this arrangement that alerted her to the fact that this was no ordinary debriefing. Before she hung up she asked him whether she could have Farsheed's things from Baku and what had happened to his body. Had he been brought home? Had he been buried properly?

'I don't know, sister. There are no things,' he said, hanging up.

She got there thirty minutes early, dressed head to toe in black, standing outside an unprepossessing residential building; one of many used by the intelligence ministry for a variety of purposes, including interviewing people. In fact, the department that Farsheed headed up, or had headed up, and where she worked was housed in such an innocuous-looking building, the many rooms converted to offices. She was met by a young woman and waited for an hour before being summoned. The questioning, by strangers, was polite at first, even friendly. They asked her about the mission in London. They asked her about the instructions she had received from Farsheed. They did not ask her how she felt about the death of Farsheed or indeed offer any condolences. This she took as a sign. After lunch Farsheed's boss came in, accompanied by a man she didn't know. The boss was the man she had spoken to from London, the very man she had often complained to in meetings, and she became aware of how vulnerable she now was without Farsheed by her side, aware that part of her bravery at challenging those in charge had come from the fact that she was Farsheed's wife. Now she was just his widow. This awareness was reinforced at the afternoon session, which was no longer about the mission in London, but turned into something else. It became about all the questions she'd ever asked, all the objections she'd ever made, all the times she'd wanted clarification about something, all the phone taps she'd questioned, the Internet traffic she'd wondered about monitoring, the things she'd said in meetings. All the things that Farsheed had both despaired of, and loved about her. She shrugged her shoulders at this line of questioning.

'Are we not allowed to question?' she asked, rhetorically.

At the end of the day a woman gave her a cardboard box with what she said were Farsheed's things in it, the things he'd had with him in Baku. At home she went through the box, but the contents were disappointingly impersonal; some programming reference books, a shoebox with some battered plastic chess pieces inside and a history book about Kūrošé Bozorg. She suspected that they'd gone through his things already, that anything of interest to them was being kept. His phone, for instance, his laptop. But who knows what disappeared with him in the car.

She looked across the room at his other chess set, one made of heavy carved pieces, with a board inlaid with mother-of-pearl. A family heirloom made in Shiraz, it was always laid out with some chess problem. She would often see him, from the comfort of the bed after lovemaking, standing naked (except for his glasses) at the board, studying it for what seemed like an eternity, until she would doze off, contented.

Sometimes when she was alone she liked to feel the heft of the pieces.

'Have you been touching the chess board again?' he would ask, mockingly stern; she obviously did not put the pieces back to his liking.

'Is it a crime,' she would respond, all innocent, 'to fondle the king in your absence?' This would provoke him into chasing her laughing into the bedroom where she would let him administer a fitting 'punishment', after which they both had to shower. Her vision blurred once again as she tried to put the plastic pieces back in their box.

The next day's interrogation moved on to conversations she'd had, or might have had, with Farsheed; the interrogators claimed they had details of their plotting. Had he relayed these conversations to his boss? Her mind reeled with the possibility that they'd been monitored. All their conversations about politics had been in open places, nothing had been committed to email, and they had confided in nobody else. No, it soon became apparent that the questions were couched only in generalities, there was nothing specific they could pin on her; they were fishing. The other man, the one she didn't know, with the groomed regulation beard and collarless suit, asked her about Farsheed. It was him they were interested in, not her, he said. Had Farsheed met with people from the opposition, or contacted pro-monarchists abroad? What were his views on reforms, or the separatist groups? Had he expressed any doubts to her? *Yes, they had consciously lived their lives in doubt*, but she said nothing, repeatedly pointing out the great things he had done for the service, for the country. How he had built up the cyber-intelligence department of the ministry. These people knew nothing. They eat their own because they constantly see any questioning from their own as a threat from the outside. It is like a disease. She grew increasingly tired but decided she would no longer be afraid.

But on the fifth day things turned more ominous. They started to ask her about what contact she'd had in London with the Mossad agent. She'd had no contact with any agents, she said, and if she had she didn't know they were agents. What about Jews, had she met any Jews in London? If she'd been a civilian she could have asked for a lawyer, for all the good it would have done. Since, however, she was working for the very people who were questioning her, she held out little hope. If only she'd had the inclination, the energy, the will to carry on, the need to carry on, she might have fought the coming battle with logic, arguments, everything at her disposal. She might still have had allies in the ministry. People liked Farsheed, they respected his work. But then Farsheed was gone and with him any hope she might have had. Any friends would keep their heads down once they knew of her fate. Being tarnished by association was a real career-ending fear.

Towards the end of the day, after repetitive questions and long periods of waiting around for them to go and confer, or eat, or have an afternoon nap – or whatever it was they were doing as she waited in the room with a barred window that had a view on to a courtyard with a fig tree growing in the middle – she was shown a photograph of Farsheed. It was in colour but grainy, she guessed, because it had been taken with a long lens. But unmistakably him, hunched over a chess board in a café opposite a large, older man with a dark moustache and greying hair.

'Do you know that man? Did you see him in London? Did you meet with him?' they pressed. No, she indicated, truthfully, by shaking her head, unable to speak, mesmerized by the photo, thinking only that they must have others which she would love to see. She could feel the tears running down her face; she hadn't wanted to cry in front of them.

'Why did they kill him? Why?'

'They killed three ministry people. Farsheed was not the one they were after, he just happened to be driving the car. The other two were more senior,' the older man said, not unkindly. She looked at the photo.

'He liked to play chess,' she said when they took it away. 'Wherever he went, he took a chess set and would play with whoever he could find.'

'He was not choosy about who he played with?' one of them asked.

'As long as they provided a good enough challenge. He rarely found people who matched his intellect,' she said, looking at Farsheed's boss, holding his gaze.

He looked away. 'We'll need to reclaim the apartment,' he said. 'It belongs to the ministry and is meant for a family, not a woman living on her own.'

FIFTY-FOUR

'I'd rather you didn't come to the house tonight, or the airport tomorrow,' Sheila said. 'Do you mind?'

Julian, who had been planning to accompany her back home and to the airport, was secretly pleased; he didn't really want to stand around watching her pack and he hated airport goodbyes, especially as the one staying behind. She had come to see his studio apartment before he moved out, just out of curiosity, she said. He'd told her, as they lay on the bed, that it felt like he'd brought a woman back to his bachelor pad.

'That's exactly what's happened. How many does that make?'

'You've just experienced the mattress – do you think I'd bring anyone back here?'

'They wouldn't come back for seconds, that's for sure.'

'Thanks.'

'I meant perhaps we should have used that chair, stupid.'

'I don't think it was built for that sort of thing.' He could smell the perfume he'd bought her every Christmas for the last

ten years. Strange he should just notice it now and not earlier.
'I'm happy not to come home or to the airport,' he said. Anyway,
as far as he was concerned, they had just said their goodbyes.
'I'm proud of you, by the way,' he said to her back as she put
on her shirt, 'for what you're doing.'

She turned to study him, her face ready in anticipation of his
mocking her.

'Really, I mean it.'

'Well, I'm bricking it,' she said, padding without underwear
to the toilet.

'You'll be fine once you're there.' Part of him was worried
– it was Afghanistan after all – but he was determined not to
fuss, and Gulnar was going with her. He trusted Gulnar to make
sure she didn't do anything stupid.

'Ooh, I forgot to tell you,' she shouted from the toilet. 'Guess
who's agreed in principle to be a patron of Standing Together?'
She flushed before he could ask and he had to wait for her to
come back in.

'Jude Law.'

'Wow, how did you wangle him?'

'Gulnar bagged him. Her partner is a film make-up artist and
guess who happened to be starring in the last film she was working
on?'

'The man himself.'

'Gulnar and I are meeting him and his people when we come
back, you know, to show them what we're planning. You'll get
to meet him at the launch if he signs up.' She pulled on her
underwear.

'Maybe he'd be interested in the story of Boris.'

'Have you heard anything about that?'

He shook his head. 'It's as if it never happened.'

'The new owners have moved in. An American family with
young kids.'

'I'm surprised you could bring yourself to go back there.'

'I thought it would be traumatic, you know, visiting the place
again. It was fine actually. It felt good putting an actual family
in there. Those toddlers running around were like an exorcism
or something. I feel sorry for him more than anything.' She sat
on the edge of the bed, stepped into her jeans then lay back and

lifted her legs to pull them over her buttocks, like a teenager. 'Did you learn anything from his diary?' she asked.

'Not really, I couldn't make sense of it all. He'd lost his faith, I think.'

'Religious faith?'

'I'm not sure he had any religious faith to start with. It's more a faith in humanity he lost. Maybe that's overstating it – maybe it was political faith, but not just in any one idea, more the ability to believe that anything was worth pursuing any more. Does that make sense?'

'Sounds like he was in a pretty dark place.' She stood up and scanned his still-naked body. He was enjoying being naked now that he was fitter. 'What about you – you haven't lost your ability to believe, have you?'

'I don't know. I'll be able to tell you when you get back.'

Three days later, with Sheila gone, Julian sat with Nizar and his friends in a pub which he had the niggling feeling he'd been in before. For some reason he'd decided to come in a linen suit, half treating it like an interview. It was a mistake; he felt over-dressed, everyone else was in jeans, trainers and T-shirts, one of which read 'Edward Snowden for Nobel Peace Prize'. He was also the only white person at the table, and twice the average age. He couldn't have been more different, yet they all had a common bond, otherwise they wouldn't be here.

Some of the five present – each a different nationality, according to Nizar – regarded him with open suspicion. One of the things he'd ascertained from Nizar before coming was whether they had some religious agenda, but was assured that they didn't, and that although two of them were Muslims (one practising), the others were Christian or, in Nizar's case, an atheist. He wondered whether he could drop something about Sheila's charity into the conversation to give himself some much-needed kudos.

When Nizar had approached him in the café, after Julian had just split the partnership and effectively dismantled many years of hard work, he had laid out a grand vision of providing secure and anonymous Internet access to those living in repressive regimes that monitored and blocked it, with a focus on the Middle East. Although he was not overly excited by the idea itself – there were already variations of it floating around – Julian had been excited by Nizar's enthusiasm. Nizar, if not the others before him now, understood their limitations, which were not just technical, but were also about people management and project planning. Nizar had given him a look at what they were doing (without their knowledge, it turned out, which partly explained the hostility) and Julian had immediately discovered several ways in which things could be improved or streamlined. Nizar had arranged this meeting to give him a chance to explain how he could help them. A job interview, Julian thought, by people half his age.

'I admire what you're trying to do,' Julian kicked off. 'It needs doing. But it needs doing properly.' Here some looks were exchanged and Julian pushed on, explaining how he could help them in terms of project management and expertise, how he could assess each of their strengths and divide the labour accordingly, with Nizar nodding all the while. There were some sceptical questions about whether they actually needed any help and some of the conversation was in Arabic, and heated. Julian decided to make things clearer.

'Look. I'm not planning to be the Lawrence of Arabia of the programming world.' He looked for smiles but saw none. 'I'm offering to be a servant to your cause, to bring you my years of experience in this area. You've got a good idea here, but it's something that could become useful everywhere. Your vision has universal appeal, so you need to think beyond the Middle East, especially with what we now know is happening in the USA and in the UK.' Here he gestured at the Edward Snowden T-shirt and glanced at Nizar, who gave a nod.

'Governments everywhere are increasingly wanting to control access to online information. But having the right approach at this early stage is going to matter later on. It will make it easier to both scale it and adapt it to changing situations. Because believe me, once you create a way to bypass state security or censorship they will plug the hole and make the virtual walls higher and thicker. What I'm saying is that it's going to be an ongoing struggle and it's something that will need to be configurable at a local level by as many people as possible. Think big, think flexible, think open source. Also, think about what the next project is going to be, and how you're going to fund the development time, 'cause nobody is going to pay you to do this.'

They looked at each other and shrugged but appeared mollified by his little speech, and Julian went to the bar to get another round of drinks while they had a discussion. As Julian waited to be served he remembered why the pub was familiar: of course he'd been in it before, many years ago, although it had changed from a smoky dive for university lecturers and PhD students to something more upmarket.

It was near Conway Hall, where Julian had attended some political rallies and heard some rousing speeches. He'd also been to his last rhetoric-filled SWP meeting there. Boris had approached him afterwards, in this very pub, telling him what a waste of time it all was and asking whether he wouldn't be interested in doing something that would have actual, real-world results. Julian had been intrigued, not least because he had frankly become lost in all the political infighting and splits, and being of a practical bent had been thinking that exact thing himself. Of course, it was easy to see now that Boris had picked up on the fact that Julian was looking for something to belong to, something bigger than himself, and had offered him entry to a secret and exclusive club. Looking across the room at the earnest young men (no women – not yet, anyway) he smiled, thinking that here was something he could belong to. Nizar came up to help him carry the beers and Cokes back to the table.

'You're in,' he said, 'but you'll need to prove yourself.'

'That, comrade, is a two-way street.'

'Fair enough.' They drank a toast, and Julian wondered whether Boris would approve of his new venture with this disparate bunch, thrown together by common cause. He liked to think he would. He picked up the drinks. 'Shall we get started?' he asked.

FIFTY-FIVE

Upon leaving the interrogation house for the last time Mojgan noticed a dusty car with its back up against the closed metal gates leading to the front of the house. A man she vaguely knew, a factotum for Farsheed's computing unit,

leant against the bonnet of the car, smoking. He was a distant
relative of Farsheed for whom he had created a job, something
she had objected to on principle. He'd told her it was a nothing
job, inconsequential, the man had no ambition, just a simpleton
whom nobody else would employ. In the back seat sat a woman
in a chador, talking and laughing into a mobile phone. The
woman, whom Mojgan recognized, was a guard at the Evin prison
and was usually dispatched to accompany female prisoners who
were being taken there. She did not acknowledge Mojgan, but
that may have been because she was on the phone. Another man,
the driver, sat behind the wheel, reading the latest copy of *Kayhan*,
the official newspaper of the hardliners; Farsheed had said it was
run by the intelligence agency.

As she passed the smoking man he smiled at her and said,
sotto voce, 'We'll pick you up in the morning.'

Without giving her time to acknowledge or question what he'd
said, he moved away as if he hadn't spoken, heading into the
building she had just emerged from. As she walked home she
understood what he was telling her.

She wasn't going back to the same interrogation house in the
morning; that was a mere five minutes' walk from her apartment,
and they wouldn't be picking her up from home for that short a
journey. Mojgan climbed the stairs to her empty apartment, her
feet heavier with every step. She had been to Evin prison many
times, before moving to the computing section, so she knew the
routine. On arrival she would be blindfolded and led to the special
women's wing run by the intelligence ministry, where she would
be placed in solitary confinement. She would seize on the smallest
kindness given by one of the female prison guards as a sign of
hope, a shared humanity. It meant that she would spend months,
possibly years, being submitted to interrogations, blindfolded
there and back. They would go back over every mission, every
perceived failure, every person she had met outside Iran. Worse
still, her relationship with Farsheed would be subjected to forensic
examination, and it was this she couldn't bear the thought of.
She opened the door and locked it behind her, drawing the bolts
across the top and bottom. She went to the bathroom cabinet,
where Farsheed kept sleeping pills that he didn't need. She'd
asked him once why he had them.

'In case I need to sleep,' was his droll answer, but maybe he had an escape route planned in the back of his mind. Maybe, if he was in the same position, without her, he would also want to sleep forever.

She made some chamomile tea and recovered his tattered book of Rumi poetry from the bedroom shelf, the corners of certain pages folded over in a way she'd told him off about. She also pulled out the plastic chess set he'd had in Baku, the one she had seen him using in the photo they'd shown her. He had been playing white, and because the pieces were one of the last things that his fingers had touched she took them out and held them to her lips, in the hope that they might transfer his physicality to her at some atomic level. She lay on the bed, propped up by embroidered cushions they had chosen together in the Grand Bazaar, the tea and pills by her side, and turned the pages of the Rumi, looking for solace, looking for something that would ease her transition. A ghazal grabbed her attention: number 911, 'On the Day of My Death'. She started to read it, swallowing pills:

> On the day of my death when my coffin is going by, don't imagine that I have any pain about leaving this world.
> Don't weep for me, and don't say. 'How terrible! What a pity!'

She took another pill, another sip of chamomile tea.

> When you see my funeral, don't say, 'Parting and separation!' Since for me, that is the time for union and meeting God.

Another pill. More tea. *The time for union and meeting God.* This wasn't what she was looking for. She wanted something that indicated she would have a union with Farsheed. She moved through the book, reaching ghazal number 1392, 'I Was Dead'.

> I was dead
> I came alive

I was tears
I became laughter

If only he had sent a message, a final message. *A message.*
An email message. The email she had sent him from the black
woman's house, on the encrypted email website: in her grief she
hadn't thought to check and see if he'd replied. Stupid, stupid
Mojgan. She got off the bed and felt her legs give way. Her
netbook was not far, in the living room, which she reached with
difficulty. Woozy, she switched it on, and the start-up sound made
her open her eyes. She logged on. Inbox: one message. It was
enough for her to drag herself to the toilet and stick her fingers
down her throat.

At the border crossing of the small town of Bazargan, Mojgan
could see 'Türkiye' neatly spelled out in stones on a hill, beck-
oning with the promise of freedom on the other side of the fence.
    She'd been relieved – two days ago now – to see the half-
digested pills emerge from her throat, along with the tea. When
nothing more came up but bile and her eyes were watering, she
made coffee. Strong coffee, lots of it, coffee as thick as syrup,
more bitter than the stuff she would soon be able to get once over
the border that she was waiting to cross. Only after emptying her
stomach and drinking her first cup had she gone back to the
computer and opened the message. It was short. But it was enough.

> I miss the curling locks of your luxurious hair, the smell
> between your creamy thighs, the glow in your cheeks as
> you envelop me, the flash in your black eyes when your
> pleasure is released.
> Remember that I am always inside you.
> As Mawlana said:
> 'Lovers do not finally meet somewhere.
> They are in each other all along.'
> Take care, my sweetheart.
> F.

They had underestimated her, that was her saving grace. Just
a woman, known only as Farsheed's wife, they would attribute

to her no independent thought, thinking she would be lost without him. 'Why did he send a woman to do a man's job?' they had asked her. They were nearly right about her being lost; she very nearly was. They had taken her Iranian passport but hadn't even thought to ask for her German passport with the Turkish name and a tourist visa for Iran issued in Frankfurt with two days left on it, which she now clutched tightly, waiting. Perhaps they didn't know about it, perhaps it was something Farsheed had organized without their knowledge, an escape hatch for just such an occasion. She was hoping this small border crossing would not be on their radar. Her hair was sheared under the chador, cut two days ago before she left her apartment building at the crack of dawn, the long strands dumped in the street so they wouldn't be found in the apartment when they came. No reason to have it long any more. She needed to travel light, and quickly, unencumbered by long, high-maintenance hair, and besides, she would not wear it long for anyone else.

Soon, God willing, she would be in Doğubeyazıt on the other side, and by tomorrow, after a tortuously long series of bus rides, in Ankara. From there she had no idea. Her future was written somewhere, she just had to discover where.

FIFTY-SIX

Julian, back from an early morning run, drinking his coffee in the kitchen while checking a news feed on his phone, came across the small item on a BBC website that referenced an article in *Popular Mechanic*. Going to his laptop, he tracked the original down, published a week ago. Iranian officials claimed to have taken control of their second drone, this one a very large, long-distance UAV which was equipped with bunker-busting weapons. There were photos with the article, but the drone looked like it was in pieces which they had tried to patch together so that it looked whole. The Iranians said they had proof that it was an Israeli UAV, unlike the US one they claimed to have taken control of a couple of years ago. There were phallic-shaped tubes with fins that looked, to Julian's untrained eye, like large bombs. The drone was huge, the size of a 737 aeroplane, and took up most of a large hangar where it sat together like a poorly constructed Airfix model. The article said that the Israelis had refused to comment on the drone but an expert in the field said it bore 'extraordinary similarity to the 4.5 ton Heron TP', which the Israeli Air Force had unveiled a year ago. He scoured the Internet for more on the story. One of the stories, in the online edition of the *New York Times*, framed it in relation to a recent cyber infection of computers at a nuclear research facility in Iran. The Iranians denied any such report, saying their cyber-defences were second to none after the Stuxnet infection of nuclear facilities in 2010. The article claimed that Iran needed a PR coup and this drone capture was a useful distraction from setbacks in that area. The new virus had been dubbed 'criss-cross' by one computer-security company. It wasn't clear who had come up with this name, but a search of the company website revealed that they had a research facility in Tel Aviv. A few minutes more and he landed on an activist website where he found a reference to the company which claimed it had 'strong links with the Israeli military and intelligence community'.

Sheila came into the kitchen, her hair tied back, in her suit. He'd suggested down-sizing their house, since his salary – now that he was just doing contract work – was intermittent and had effectively been halved, but she said she'd already paid off the mortgage so he didn't need to worry about it and could do what he needed to do. She was still keeping her financial situation close to her chest, but he wasn't going to complain.

She poured herself coffee from the pot he'd made. 'Working already?'

'Just trying to find out what the news isn't actually telling me.'

'It's like a bloody iceberg,' she said, fetching a bowl and cereal. 'Most of it is hiding under the surface.'

'What are your plans today?' he asked. He felt buoyant after what he'd just read.

'A possible house sale this morning, then this afternoon Gulnar and I give a presentation to a group of occupational therapists, to try to convince them that they should go to work in a war zone. Listen, don't forget Gulnar and her partner are coming round for dinner. You're cooking, right?'

'Yes, it's all sorted.'

'Her partner's vegetarian.'

'Stop worrying, I haven't forgotten.'

'Sorry. I'm nervous about the presentation.'

'You'll be fine, babe, you've done it before.' He cleared his throat to change down a gear. 'Remember Boris?'

She stopped eating and looked up, worry on her face. 'What is it? Has something happened?'

'No, not at all. Sorry, there's nothing to worry about. It's just that, well, I think he did a good thing.'

FIFTY-SEVEN

The chess pieces are chipped plastic and unsatisfyingly hollow. Their battleground of folding cardboard has frayed corners and the glued-on paper surface is coming away. There is a cup stain right in the centre, where the pieces now vie for control. Two men, one obviously older than the other, study the board intently, occasionally touching a piece without moving it. The bespectacled younger man, Farsheed, unconsciously flaunts the impatience of his youth, looking around the noisy and smoke-filled café, studying the other chess players. He has the air of a player who already knows what he is going to play and is frustrated at the convention of having to wait his turn. The older man, named Boris, is more circumspect. Neither of them, strictly speaking, should be consorting, even under the innocent-looking cover of a chess game in a very public chess café in Baku, of all places. But neither man seems to care, or perhaps they feel it is worth the risk. This is, after all, their third game together. Boris tentatively plays a rook, keeping a forefinger on it until he is sure of his move. He hits the clock as soon as he does, then strokes his moustache thoughtfully. Farsheed whips his piece across the board, replacing the rook with one of his own. He puts it next to some others on the table, arranging them in order of importance: pawns, knight, and now a rook. He does all this before stopping his clock, as if he has time to burn or is just showing Boris that he doesn't care about how much time remains on his clock. Boris plays more quickly this time, and there is a small flurry of pieces exchanged and clock hitting. They sit back briefly, contemplating the now sparsely populated board. Boris leans forward, Farsheed does the same, unconsciously echoing him. Their heads are just inches apart.

'There is a man,' Farsheed says in English, without looking up, 'responsible for the security at a certain research facility. But his personal security is not so good. He connects to the Internet using the same same computer he uses on the local network.' He looks up to see if Boris is listening but he seems intent on the board. 'Anyway, he visits certain websites, bad ones, every day to download videos and pictures. He even gets some sent by email, to an account he has online. A man as devoted to God as this man says he is should not be watching such videos.' It is not Farsheed's first language, English, neither is it that of Boris, but they both speak it fairly well – Boris perhaps better than Farsheed – and both tainted with the inflections of their respective Russian and Farsi tongues.

'That is why I am not devoted to God,' Boris says, his eyes flitting between the pieces on the board, 'so I do not suffer such religious qualms.' The young man looks up, but he does not get a response in kind.

'I'm sorry to hear that. I thought you were religious.'

'No,' Boris says, shaking his head.

'I see. Is that why you are doing this? Because you have lost your religion?'

'Something is lost, but not religion. Something more fundamental.'

Farsheed shakes his head, seemingly confused. 'So anyway,' he asks, 'you can do something with this knowledge?'

'Of course I can, but I need an IP address,' Boris says.

Farsheed smiles and shakes his head. 'When I have verified your side of the bargain, then I will make an email address available to you immediately, not an IP address; you know, an IP address can be linked to a geographical location, so I cannot provide that. Anyway, this man subscribes to certain videos using this email address, do you understand?'

Boris nods and moves a pawn up the right flank. 'It needs to be a video that he is guaranteed to look at, so I need more detail about his specific interests, so we can tailor it, make it appealing to him.'

Farsheed nods, making a mirror-image move on the board, but says nothing. Instead he takes off his glasses and proceeds to clean them with the napkin taken from under his glass of tea.

'So what is it?' Boris asks. 'Lesbians? Oral? Gangbangs? Anal?'

Farsheed blushes and, even though Boris is speaking softly, looks around before putting his glasses back on.

'Please tell me it's not underage girls?' Boris asks.

Farsheed shakes his head and studies the board very carefully. It must be obvious to Boris that he cannot say it. Boris sighs, perhaps worried that he is going to have to run through every sexual fetish before they get anywhere useful. Farsheed glances at a nearby table where a young boy sits on his father's lap, watching him play chess. Then he looks back at Boris, his glasses reflecting the sunlight from outside, then to the boy, then down at the board, then back to Boris.

'No?' Boris says, raising his eyebrows. 'Really?'

Farsheed nods, seemingly ashamed, as if he is somehow tainted by the sordid perversions of a compatriot.

'OK. That is definitely something that can be used.'

'But after this,' Farsheed says, gesturing at the board, 'there can be no more contact. No direct exchange, no phone calls, no texts, nothing online. Online is not safe. And if you try to be safe you immediately look suspicious.'

'I'm old school, as they say.'

'Old school?'

'Old-fashioned. I like to hold things in my hand, to look into someone's eyes, to hear what they have to say. I like physical indicators that things have happened.' He moves another pawn.

'What about your side of the bargain?' the young man asks.

'Yes, of course. Let's talk about that.'

'It sounds more complicated.'

'I am giving you more than an email address, my young friend.'

'Yes, I understand. You are giving me an opportunity, like I am giving you an opportunity. That is all we are doing.'

'Agreed. But the opportunity I am giving you has a potentially bigger reward for you, as well as a bigger risk for me, which is why it is more complicated for you. You will need to work harder for it. I will do what I can do make it easy but I am dealing in unknowns.'

The young man shrugs, and it's not clear whether it's because he doesn't agree with the assertion that it is complicated or that it provides a bigger payback. 'So what will you give me?'

'A name. That's all. An opportunity.'

'When does this happen?' asks the young man.

'I travel tomorrow.'

'Tomorrow?' the young man asks, surprised.

'It is now or never. I'll be gone for four weeks. I need a week to set things up, then you can take your opportunity.'

'Yes.'

'Your deadline, your window of opportunity, will end exactly midnight today in four weeks, do you understand?'

'I understand.'

'Repeat it.'

'I got it. Four weeks today. That's August the fifteenth at midnight.'

'And will you be going yourself?'

'No, I am unable to leave. I am sending someone.'

'You can trust this person? They know about me?'

'Yes, I can trust them, it is someone very close to me. But she does not know about you.'

'Her? You're sending a woman?'

Farsheed blushes at his amateurish error. 'I am sending the best person I know.'

'Fine, as long as she knows what is needed?'

Farsheed nods.

'Listen, if you are staying you should continue to come back here, continue to play chess,' Boris says, smiling. His teeth are stained from past smoking; he has not smoked at any of the games. 'You'll have time to improve your game.'

'In four weeks? Four years is not enough time to improve my game.' Farsheed moves a bishop down the board but it is a stalling move, the outcome is clear. 'So how will I get this name?'

'I'll tell you it in a minute,' Boris says, and, seeing the young man's surprise, adds, 'I told you, I'm old school, and I don't want any paper or electronic record of this information passing between us. For that reason you should remember it and tell it to whoever you are sending. No writing it down, no electronic footprints. You understand? The same applies to the email address you give me afterwards.'

Farsheed smiles. Then he frowns. 'But how to get it to you at the end? There can be no meeting with the person I am sending.'

'No, of course not. She will have to pass it to me somehow, by midnight on the fifteenth. I will not be around after then.'

Farsheed nods and moves a piece. He is an adequate player, judging by previous games, but these conditions are not ideal for concentration. In fact, he looks likely to be beaten in a few moves, four at most. To his credit, he realizes it. He picks up his king and lays it on its side, stopping the clock. He holds out his hand to mark the traditional end to a chess game. 'Good game,' he says, as they shake hands.

They stare at the position on the board for a few seconds, as if to discern some meaning that they have overlooked.

'What about you? Why are you doing this?' Boris asks.

Farsheed removes his glasses and looks up, squinting, thinking. 'Sometimes, when everyone treats someone as if they are a criminal, they can start to behave like one, especially if nobody believes that they are innocent. They think, why not be a criminal, there is no benefit to not being one. It is like a prophecy that comes true because you behave in a way that makes it true. I don't explain it very well, perhaps?'

'No, I understand. It's a self-fulfilling prophecy.'

'Self-fulfilling,' Farsheed repeats, nodding.

'Hadfish Systems, in London,' Boris says. 'Repeat it.'

'Hadfish Systems.'

Boris nods and stands up. 'Good luck.'

'I think luck should not be a factor.'

'Luck is always a factor, comrade. The trick is to adapt to it.'

Outside, Boris looks back into the café and watches the handsome young man, just a boy really, sitting at the table and sweeping his chess pieces into a battered shoe box on his lap.